THOMAS'S NEED

A Quidell Brothers
ROMANCE

The coolness of his skin surprises me. He's usually so much warmer than me, with his energy-consuming, muscular body, but working out here shirtless all night has left a chill in his bones.

He can't be this way. Not my Tom. The cold steals his charm and his wit; it takes away his ability to see in the world what needs to be seen. It closes him off and...

I press my face into his shoulder. I hold on for dear life. And I can't help but wonder if this time, I need to rescue him....

THOMAS'S NEED

Quidell Brothers Book 4

KRIS AUSTEN RADCLIFFE

Six Love Erotic Romance

THE WORLDS OF
KRIS AUSTEN RADCLIFFE

THOMAS'S NEED

A Quidell Brothers
ROMANCE

By
Kris Austen Radcliffe

Six Love Erotic Romance
Minneapolis

www.krisaustenradcliffe.com

Published by
Six Love Erotic Romance

Edited by Annetta Ribken
Copyedited by Juli Lilly
Cover to be designed by Kris Austen Radcliffe
Plus a special thanks to my Proofing Crew.

For requests, please e-mail: publisher@sixtalonsign.com.

Third print edition, June 2018
Version: 6.25.2018

ISBN: 978-1-939730-66-4

THOMAS'S NEED

A Quidell Brothers
ROMANCE

CHAPTER 1

Thomas

"Put this on, Uncle Tommy." Bart holds out a child-sized, bark-brown vest complete with child-sized arm holes and a child-sized bug "abdomen" hanging off its back. "You can't go in unless you're an ant like me."

My nephew tugs on his own vest before looking up at me with his big, blue, five-year-old eyes.

Kids are exhausting. We've been in the Children's Museum for just over an hour and I already want to run for the hills, or for a beer. Either would work. But I promised my brother's boy an afternoon of "fun in the city" so here we are, a happy-if-precise kindergartener and his big oaf of an uncle, at the mouth of an indoor "anthill" play tunnel.

This particular exhibit has been a staple of the Children's Museum since I was a child. Hell, I think it was here when Bart's grandfather was a child. It was probably here before Minneapolis became a city. The first human to step onto this spot fifteen thousand years ago slammed a spear into the ground and declared, "Let's build the kids an anthill right here!"

Some things never change, including the murals rolling over the costume area where Bart now stands, and the air around us. An odd mixture of aged dust, cleaning chemicals, and that specific, sweet-yet-sour scent of child hangs in the air as thick as the shadows deep in the tunnels.

I run a finger over the pockmarked paint. Refreshing the blues in the mural would go a long way to adding a little brightness.

Funny how I never noticed the blandness of the colors when I was the kid playing. I just wanted to run fast and lose my younger brother inside the tunnels. It never worked; Rob always lost *me*. I suspect Bart would do the same.

I point at the vest. "I don't think that'll fit, buddy."

Bart frowns. He's already taller than all the other five-year-olds and I suspect he's destined for the full Quidell height and broad build, like his father and his uncles. Small we are not, which is fine, except when you're supposed to crawl through an insect mound.

"Oh." Bart's hand—and the vest—drop to his side. He looks at the floor for a moment, then out into the open area in front of the exhibit, his face open and hopeful. "Auntie Sammie can come in with me!"

My fiancé looks up from her task of stuffing Bart's action figures into his backpack. "What?" She smooths the front of her t-shirt as she stands up.

Sammie is slightly older than me—four years to be exact. She graduated from the University the same year I started. We'd crossed paths as students, but only in a disconnected, lost-opportunity kind of way. Thankfully, we met again last year when I started in the Art Department where we both work.

We've been making up for lost time ever since.

Her t-shirt hugs her curves, as do her jeans. Sammie's perfect female shape and luminescent auburn hair set her apart from the tired parents herding little ones through the exhibits. In my eyes, she's a vision.

But she doesn't seem as overwhelmed by the noise as I am. Sammie, unlike me, understands how to replenish her reservoir of energy.

"Bart would like you to be an ant with him." I point at my nephew. He smiles.

Sammie's face takes on an *Oh my God you are so adorable* look. The one every human with a soul makes when in the presence of kids or kittens. That wide-eyed pout, the one that only flits across features because everyone knows adults don't make that face.

But it's hard not to, when a kindergartener wants you to play.

And I think I fall even more in love with Sammie than I was after our quality cuddle time this morning, if that's even possible.

A little girl with golden skin and equally golden eyes runs around Sammie's side. Her big, curly ponytail bounces as she darts by me and right up to Bart.

"Hello," says the little girl. She's his height, which means she's probably slightly older than him, and she obviously knows her way around.

Bart doesn't say anything. He just stares all dumbfounded at the pretty girl.

Sammie's gaze shifts from Bart to me. She shakes her head as she walks over.

The little girl takes the ant-vest from my nephew's hand. "I'll be an ant with you."

Bart smiles a new, big, happy smile. "Okay."

The little girl slips the vest over her shoulders. "This way gets to the slide faster." She points behind me, then looks up at my face. "Are you his daddy?"

"That's my uncle," Bart says. He steps between his new friend and me as if I'm competition. "He's an artist."

I can't help but chuckle.

Bart throws me a look, but when the girl takes his hand, he's utterly, completely lost.

"Let's go!" she says, and my nephew disappears into the anthill with his new friend.

Sammie sets the backpack at our feet and leans her head against my shoulder. "Ah, young love."

I take her hand as I watch an older woman guide my young nephew through the tunnels. At least Bart didn't miss *his* chances.

I kiss Sammie's cheek. "I guess he's better at seeing his opportunities than his uncle."

Sammie looks up at my face. Her brows twist up for a second, and her warm, hazel eyes take on a shadow. But she shakes her head again and pats my elbow. "What's that saying? You make your own opportunities?"

"Yeah," I say, and kiss her cheek again. She's my muse, my Sammie. What would I do without her?

⚜

"HER NAME IS SERENA!" BART KICKS THE BACK OF SAMMIE'S SEAT.

There's not a lot of room in the back of my truck's cab. Sammie waves her hand over the headrest. "Watch the toes, please," she says.

Bart ignores her. He's too wrapped up in his cougar moment. "Like the tennis player." Bart swings his arm. "How do you play tennis, Uncle Tommy?" He swings his arm again. "Serena says she plays tennis and volleyball. She knows how to ski down hills!"

He makes a loud *whooshing* noise. Sammie throws me a bemused look.

Bart leans forward. "Can I learn to ski? I want to ski." His next noise sounds more like a monster truck than the swishing of snow.

I turn into my brother's neighborhood. It's nice—suburban and full of mature trees and well-maintained, middle-class split-levels. Dan says the schools are good and the streets safe. The area reminds me a lot of our neighborhood growing up, which, I suspect, is why he chose to buy a house here.

That's my brother, the painfully perfect family man.

"I think we've created a monster." Sammie nods over her shoulder.

Bart continues his monologue about the wide range of sporting activities available to today's youth.

The truck's engine grumbles one last time as I park in Dan's driveway. Dan's girlfriend, Camille, steps out onto the front step. She's freshly showered. Her damp black hair hangs over her shoulders and her muscles look loose as if she just finished a good workout.

"I think you and Camille need to pose for me." A full suite of classic painterly poses run through my head. "I could do a full series. Call it 'The Muses.'"

Sammie smiles as she opens the door and steps out. She helps Bart undo his seatbelt and he's running for Camille before I pull the key from the ignition.

Sammie taps the side panel of the truck as she watches him go. "I think he had fun."

I walk around the front of the truck and wrap my arms around her waist. "How could he not?" I gently kiss her upper lip. "He's a Quidell. We have a weakness for cougars."

Sammie slaps my shoulder. "Me-*ow*," she says, and saunters up the driveway, toward my brother's house.

I chuckle as I follow.

"Concert's at nine," she says over her shoulder.

We had an afternoon with the nephew. Now it's time to party like adults. I will never understand where Sammie gets the energy for it all.

Other than she sleeps better than I do. But I made a promise, so I smile. "We'd better get home so we can get ready."

Sammie's eyes brighten. Her hips swing as she follows Bart. She holds her back erect and her shoulders high, but her head tips just a little to the side as she takes in how Camille hugs Bart.

And again, I think I'm more in love now than I was this morning, even if I am tired.

My Sammie. My muse. I follow her into my brother's house for a quick good-bye with Bart.

I watch my nephew run off for a cookie and a juice box.

Sammie grasps my hand. "Ready?" she asks.

I guess it's time for a whole other anthill. I kiss her again. Any night with Sammie is special, concert or no concert. "Let's go."

CHAPTER 2

Samantha

The second opening act blasts out yet another deafening electronic sample. Their singer slowly wisps her fingers through the air as if following a delicate butterfly made of sound.

The stage is cluttered and the singer is boxed in between two electronic pianos and a drum kit. Colored lights wink on and off. She trills into the microphone, swings her arms again, and wiggles her hips.

I can't remember the band's name. Not that it matters; we came for Barston Flood, the main act. The two teenagers next to us seem overjoyed and excited by the butterfly-catching move, though.

Tom's doing his best to not take up space. The venue is standing-room-only so we stayed off to the side. He didn't want to block anyone's view with his broad shoulders so he's trying to blend into a pillar, but his white shirt and his big biceps make him stand out no matter where we are.

My fiancé frowns and looks more like a bouncer than a concert-goer.

I rub his forearm and lean close to his ear. "No frowny faces."

Tom chuckles and pulls me into his arms. "Thank you for this." He nods toward the band on the stage. "She's not too bad."

I don't necessarily agree, but that's not the point. "You're welcome." I kiss his cheek and go back to listening to the fluttering waif behind the real bouncers.

Smoke drifts off the stage. Lights flash and teenagers dance. Tom rubs his eyes and watches the crowd, and the frown reappears. I can't tell if it's the dirty air or the young people that makes him itch.

He has only half a decade on most of them, yet he's making a dad face.

Sometimes I don't like being reminded that I'm older than him. Not that four years means anything, really. But when he acts like an old man, it makes me feel ancient.

He wasn't like this when we met. He was wide-eyed and fresh off the University farm, a big, smiling guy with a big heart and a knack for seeing the truth about people. If it wasn't for him, I'd still be living with my cheating ex and getting myself off on old fantasies. He helped me see the truth of my life, and he gave me the support I needed to move beyond the cage I'd built for myself.

The frowning started after his gallery show. He sold two paintings —a good start, I told him—but I think he expected better. Or, more precisely, better of himself. All his work should be exceptional all the time, and to all people, right? I think he understands intellectually how defeatist that thought is, but I also think it's still infecting his heart.

I lean against his arm and he drops a hand to my waist. The music rolling off the stage is now too loud to talk over, anyway—except I need to pee and going during the boring opening act seems like the best use of my concert-going time.

I tip up my chin and lean close to his ear again. "I need to hit the little girl's room."

He blinks as he tries to figure out what I just said. Then he grins and nods. "Grab a couple of waters on the way back, if you would, my lady."

"Aye, my handsome knight, I shall return to you bearing fluid gifts."

Again, he takes a moment to process. His grin turns into a full, wonderful smile. The kind he used to make all the time, but now seems to be hidden away under some weight neither of us can fully see or hear. He feels it, though.

"Don't lose our spot." I kiss his shoulder. We might be off to the side, but we're close to the stage.

He nods one last time and I slide away into the crowd. People brush against me, and one drunk woman giggles when she steps on my toes. Mostly, they ignore me. When the crowd thins out, I glance over my shoulder. Tom's big frame is still easy to pick out against the pillar. He's gone back to watching the stage. At least for a moment, I can believe that he's enjoying himself.

The lower level is quiet but the silence is as deafening as the beat from upstairs. The difference weighs over the room and the bar so thickly my brain has no choice but to become conscious of it.

A couple sneaks out of the women's room as I go in. They look at me with a mixture of guilt and defiance, and scuttle away as if they're afraid I'm going to tell on them.

Let them fuck in the restroom. I don't care. But if you're going to bust the rules, at least own your behavior. Don't slink away like a pair of naughty puppies.

Right after I graduated from the University, I had a boyfriend who liked semi-public sex. Fingers found their way under tablecloths and into my naughty bits. No coat room or bathroom was safe. I stopped wearing panties solely to grant him fast, smooth access.

We lasted six months. I think we both realized that it was all about the fucking, and for him, only fucking one woman at a time made the fucking less fun.

At least he had the decency to be honest about his desires. And at least I had the backbone to move on.

I stop at the bar on the way out of the restroom. I lean against its retro metal edging as I pull a couple of bills out of my clutch. "Two waters."

The bartender takes my cash and sets two ice-cold plastic bottles on the also-retro, bright-red Formica of the bar's surface. The stools gleam all chrome and bright red pleather, and the entire brightly-lit area reminds me more of a romanticized 50s-era set than an actual functioning bar.

I adjust my bag's thin strap and tuck it under my arm. The beat from upstairs rattles the bar stools and I suspect the second act is about to leave the stage. Time to return to Tom with my gifts of cool, liquidy goodness.

"Sam?"

I look up.

Standing on the steps up to the main floor is a man who I haven't seen in five years. He looks the same as he did that day during my final year at the University—expensive tailored shirt, expensive tailored pants, unmarred expensive shoes. His blue-black hair is the same well-tailored, expensive cut.

We met at a job fair. I was looking for a job and he was offering. Our affair was entirely inappropriate. Ultimately, I got the job I'm still in—working communications for a major food multi-national. He, I suspect, hired exactly what he wanted.

Because that was Juri Olson, son of the great Carl Olson, our state's most influential philanthropist, industrialist, and all-around rich guy. Carl always gets his way. Between his charm and his money, Juri does too.

He grins and extends his hand to shake mine. "How have you been, Sam?"

Juri calls me Sam. Never Sammie. Never Samantha. Always Sam. I grip his hand and shake once.

He's still the same oddly-handsome he was the six months we fucked. Same straight nose and high cheekbones. He hasn't changed, or aged, or anything, and looks my age, not the seventeen years my senior he is. He watches me with his odd, reddish-brown eyes. His irises are almost the exact same color as my hair. He used our color connection as an excuse to keep me close.

His skin carries the same warm reddish-golden tones as his eyes. They clash with the blues in his hair and make it difficult *not* to look at him. He's oddly enthralling. For a second, I wonder if Juri's a vampire.

"How are you?" he says. The pitch of his voice drops as he speaks the "you" the same way it always dropped when he wanted a blowjob.

Unlike Tom, Juri isn't much taller than me. He's not much wider at the shoulders, either, but he is wiry and a lot stronger than one would expect. I once saw him move an entire bed by himself.

I pull my hand back. "Good, Juri. And you?" Best to keep it businesslike. Juri might be the ex who liked semi-public fucks, but he was never a dick about it. Most of the time.

He slides onto one of the stools. "Doing well." He signals to the bartender. "Cabernet, please."

The bartender scurries away.

"I don't know if you heard, but we bought a chain of destination resorts." He leans against the bar. It's hard for me to believe that this man is in his forties. He shows no gray in his hair. His body still ripples under his perfectly-cut clothes. The lack of wrinkles also makes me think it must be good to be rich.

Or maybe like Tom, Juri was blessed with good genes. His mother is a Ukrainian beauty queen, so anything's possible.

"I'm in charge of the merger." He takes his cab from the bartender. "I'm here scouting." He winks and takes a sip.

Scouting? "For what?" I ask.

He shrugs. "A couple of the properties are in Nevada. One's on the Vegas Strip." He nods toward the steps. "The band intrigues me."

Bullshit, I think. I don't know why. Juri isn't a liar.

"I am currently without a trusted assistant to do the scouting for me." He shrugs and I swear he's thinking *Time for another job fair*.

But, again, Juri isn't a liar. Or a dick. Most of the time. So any double meaning I'm reading into his facial expressions is just that, me reading in something that's likely not there. Besides, Barb, his executive assistant, would have hired someone if Juri really did want the help.

"Sounds like you need a new sidekick."

Juri grins and tips his cabernet toward me before taking a sip.

He is good at multitasking and he does like his "tasks" young. Where better to find someone equal parts sweet, naughty, and smart but at a Barston Flood concert, an indie band known for their sweet, naughty, and smart lyrics?

I laugh and shake my head. "It's been good seeing you, Juri." I pick up the two water bottles.

"You are here with someone." He watched the bottles, not my face.

I hold out my hand to show him the sapphire on my finger. "Fiancé."

Juri chuckles and slaps his thigh. "You never seemed like the marrying kind, Sam." He takes another sip of his cab.

I salute with one of the bottles. "You neither, Juri." And with that, I walk up the stairs, fully aware that a very rich man is watching as I leave him behind.

CHAPTER 3

Thomas

I shouldn't be jealous. Sammie's weirded out by her encounter with her ex. She didn't tell me so, or show it in her movements, but she's blinking too fast and she can't seem to decide if she wants to lean against my side or stand three feet away.

Barston Flood is about to take the stage. The lights drop and the music leaps and all of a sudden, I can't see Sammie—just flashing lights, shadows, and ready-to-gyrate teen girls.

My brain runs with the contorted visuals and calls up an image of a coyote stalking Sammie from the smoke-filled recesses of the venue. An ingenious coyote with the means to insulate himself from the noises and the prying eyes of the world. A very rich, stealthy coyote who can take whatever he wants whenever he wants it.

Sammie looks up at my face. She squints slightly, then backs up against my front and pulls my arms around her waist.

I can't tell if she's upset or dancing. Or maybe I can't tell if *I'm* upset or dancing.

Did Juri Olson scare her? She doesn't seem frightened, but he is a rich guy and rich guys have sneaky ways to scare women.

What if I'm wrong? What if the *other* thought my brain keeps whispering is correct? What if she's upset because he's rich and a better choice and she just realized how much of a fool she's been for spending this past year with me?

Which is stupid.

I still want to punch him for talking to my fiancé—which weirds *me* out, because I'm not a Neanderthal.

The speakers rumble. The lights drop again. More smoke rolls off the stage and I steel myself for the main act's coming acoustic onslaught.

Juri Olson is seventeen years older than her and I'm four years younger which means she used to have sex with a guy who could be my father. But not *my* dad, because my dad isn't rich. Juri Olson isn't "normal" rich, either. He's super-rich, the "I can buy countries" level of rich. He's got a daughter, too. I think she's at one of the super-expensive schools out east. His daughter is an undergrad. I've been out of school a year. His daughter is closer to my age than Sammie is.

Maybe Sammie's weirded out because I'm weirded out. Or maybe she realizes she used to fuck a goddamned modern princeling. How can I *not* be jealous of *that*?

Barston Flood's drummer bounds onto the stage. I like them. I like them a lot, to be honest. I often listen to their music while I paint. But now I'm just weirded the fuck out.

The princeling's here somewhere, playing coyote. I glance up at the balcony. Is he up there, looking down at all his minions? Is he behind the bar?

Does he own this place?

I have no fucking clue. His family owns stores and warehouses and at least three small brewpubs. Hotels. Their own shipping company. He might own the whole goddamned block.

Shit, maybe they're going to buy the company Sammie and I work for and lay us all the fuck off. I heard the rumors. Not that Juri Olson had anything to do with it.

Sammie used to sleep with him.

She frowns up at me, then points at the stage. The band's two guitarists enter and the teenagers around us go wild. When the lead singer leaps onto the stage, the already epic energy level of the venue erupts.

I pull Sammie flush against my front. She's tense. She shouldn't be tense. We're having a good time. We should be enjoying the music.

And each other.

She doesn't need me acting jealous. She doesn't need an ex getting into her space, either.

Drums thump. The lead singer jumps and dances. Guitars scream. Sammie's unease drains away but mine only throbs with the beat. It works itself into my muscles and I begin to wonder if a bubble just burst. If, perhaps, the glittering sheen of my charmed life may have just ruptured.

If it was still intact, I wouldn't know about it, would I? You only miss something when it's gone.

But is it gone? "Charmed" is relative. But for some reason, knowing Sammie has exes other than that douche-nugget cheater she was with before me makes our whole relationship seem more *real*. More grounded in the actual world. She's perfect and special and a dream come true, but it's not that simple. Nothing's ever simple and I'm an idiot for thinking that the world's textures are limited only to the brush strokes and paint splatters I add to it.

Why *this* ex-boyfriend—why now, while listening to a band with a lot more talent than I have—does the truth need to slap me upside the head? Why can't I just enjoy the moment?

I kiss the top of Sammie's ear. She looks up at me, her face happy and excited, and she smiles.

Whatever my problem is, it can wait. Acrid fireworks dust clings to my tongue, but I tighten my arms again. My fiancé snuggles in. We sway and dance, and I'm going to give her this moment.

Because I can do that. Bubbles burst and ex-boyfriends appear. But I can give her the evening of joy she deserves.

I DREAM, PERHAPS. THERE WAS FUMBLING INTO BED. THERE WAS

snoring through the smoke coating my throat. We had a good time at the concert, but I *dream*.

In the dream, I wonder about the unending scenes of suffocating, prehistoric ferns and the crowd-packed, airport-concourse-like shopping malls inhabiting my head. I wonder about the rough, sandy textures I see but cannot touch and the smooth, gleaming surfaces that radiate heat and cold simultaneously.

But mostly I wonder about the colors.

The ancient ferns unfurling above my head gleam with layers of opulent greens and blues. The signs in my rat-race malls glow with the red-orange fires of a searing underworld.

Why is it that my mind makes the correct tones in a dream but I can't make them on a canvas? God knows I try. I try every day. It's my job to try.

I open my eyes to the thick darkness spread like syrup across the bedroom ceiling. The concert's smoky grit still smothers my tongue and my corneas and my eyelids carry the extra weight that puffiness always brings. Tomorrow at work I'm going to look like I went on a bender; there's no way around it.

Water pounds the loft walls and stomps on the roof. A line of storms moved in just as we drove home, and should, hopefully, clear the evening's heat. A slice of wiggling, jiggling bluish glow flashes bright and white around the curtains. I count—two, three, four...

Thunder shakes the building. The window vibrates.

After the concert, we stumbled into the loft, laughing and kissing, soaked from the storm's downpour. I dried her shoulders. She toweled off my hair. We fell into bed too tired to do anything other than sleep. Tomorrow's a work day, and we both need our jobs. Someone has to pay for the loft's bamboo flooring.

Sammie's weirded-out vibe stopped halfway through the band's first set. Mine did not, though having a beautiful woman dancing with me and holding my hand went a long way toward helping me to forget the worries of my world.

Then I slept. I should know better than to sleep. I dream.

When I was a kid, I'd wake up yelling. No reason why, no real sense of dread, just a sense of vividness. My father would tell me my dreaming brain knew I was destined for greatness and it was just practicing yelling over the inevitable roar of my adoring fans.

My mother would roll her eyes and tuck me in.

Then she and my sister died in a car crash.

My lower back tightens into a hard rock of pain. My elbows do as well—I don't know why—and it flares up into my shoulders and down into my fingers. There's not a lot I can do about my random pains other than get up and work them out. Running helps. Painting often helps, and is a better idea than running in the middle of the night.

Sammie tries to help. She's the reason I try. I'm still surprised she wants to marry me, especially now that she's been reminded of her other, better options.

The streetlight below our window casts wavering rain patterns onto the ceiling through the open slit between the curtains. A truck rumbles by. Dampness weighs down the air with the slight ozone, wet fly-zapper smell that comes with summer thunderstorms, even with the air conditioner running.

I like living in Uptown. I do, but the city noise never backs off here. Not at three in the morning. Not in a thunderstorm. Our home over the shops floats above ever-present humanity. Sometimes I wish we could move to my family's lake cabin permanently.

Sammie sighs into her pillow and rolls away, and the sliver of light from the window—the same silver slice of rain-dabbled blue playing along the ceiling—cuts across her shoulder.

Her skin glows.

All I want is to crawl under the blanket and spoon against her back. Lay a kiss on that shoulder, then another on her neck, below the low braid she wears her lush hair in during the night. A third kiss, perhaps, just under her earlobe, on the spot I know makes her shiver.

I've woken her up for cuddles and sex before. I could do it again. The slow, steady pressure of my cock against the sweet roundness of her ass and my finger against her clit usually builds to her waking up so horny she's riding me before she realizes she's awake.

It would be a nice distraction from the dreams.

Her braid falls over her shoulder blades and the bedcovers, to her waist. Carefully, I brush aside enough of the blanket to reveal the gentle curve of her lower back.

The cat meows.

Our buff-colored, slightly tabby ball of fur jumps onto the bed. Mr. Pickles—Mickles, to the world—stands on my pillow staring at me with his golden-green kitty eyes as if I'm the dumbest kitten he's ever had to teach to hunt.

"What do you want?" I mumble.

"*Meoh?*" My fiancé's cat taps my cheek with his paw. He purrs and does his excited cat foot-lifting dance.

"You found another mouse, didn't you?" He might be a mound of buff-colored fluff, but he's turned out to be an agile mouser. Three months in the new loft and the cat's killed at least a dozen mice. The fat, squeaky little bastards seem to think our home is a better choice than the shop downstairs.

Mickles jumps off the bed but stops at the bedroom door to wait for me to follow. His light-colored fur luminesces in the shimmer leaking in around the curtains and he stands out against the shadows of the hallway. Mr. Pickles, the great fluffy ghost hunter.

He meows.

"I'm coming," I whisper. I tug on my sleep pants and tiptoe into the loft's short hallway. Mickles slinks ahead of me, his fat tail straight out from his body and his belly close to the floor, determined to share the thrill of the hunt with his big, bipedal kitten.

Once something catches the cat's attention, he doesn't give up— much like Sammie. We've been together a little over a year and she's already set up a gallery show of my work, and is determined to set up another, this time in California.

She also wants to rep my younger brother's girlfriend's photography career, and she's been instrumental in setting up marketing for my older brother's company. My fiancé is a dynamo.

As is Mickles. For an old cat, he's spry. He slinks down the hall and into our wide, open studio-slash-entertainment area. Out here, I leave the curtains open, and the rain-splattered reflections dance over his fur as he cat-jogs on by and into the kitchen. He immediately darts toward the pantry door.

"You know it's probably gone by now." I need to talk to the guys running the software start-up downstairs again. Mouse-proofing the building will only work if they pitch in.

Mickles meows and paws at the door. Slowly, I pull it open. He darts in, an arrow of predatory feline death, only to trot out moments later forlorn and empty-jawed.

"Told you." I pick him up and rub his ears. "Thanks for trying, fluffy dude."

His purrs meld into the thunder. I pad out of the kitchen, past our big, "upcycled" dining room table, and under the arch leading into my studio area.

It was here, in the dead of winter, that Sammie and I made love on the abandoned desk the previous occupants left behind. Right where I stand now in a puddle of red and blue light thrown by the shop sign across the street. Now, my drafting table sits where the desk used to be. My easel stands closer to the window, but I keep my brushes, paints, inks, and other supplies in a wide cabinet close to the stairs leading down to the loft's door. Several canvases, some painted, some not, line the wall, and Sammie's added jewel-toned fabrics and a few candles.

Sammie found this place. This space felt perfect then. It still does.

I set down Mickles. He rubs my leg once, then strolls off toward the kitchen, most likely to hold kitty vigil in front of the pantry door for the rest of the night.

I glance at our dark bedroom door. Sammie sleeps alone in there.

The thunder and lightning have let up, and the rain slides down the window instead of pounding at it like a horde of hammers.

The sign across the street winks and a pulse of green dances through my studio. I glance at the naked canvas sitting on my easel and I can't *not* think about my dream colors. About the layers of greens and blues shared between the suffocating prehistoric ferns and the flashes of shop signs.

I switch out the canvas for drawing paper. Sammie needs something to rep, doesn't she?

It's dark and it's night, but all I can do is try.

CHAPTER 4

Samantha

My phone's alarm chirps and I flop over. My hand pats along the mattress before I'm fully awake—before I open my eyes to the sunshine snaking around the curtains and into the bedroom. My fingers should find Tom sprawled on his belly next to me, naked and morning-gorgeous, his hair a mess and the hard muscles of his back rippling and perfect.

Instead, Mickles licks my fingers.

I open my eyes to the vast, empty landscape of our king-size bed to find the dunes of our bunched up blankets inhabited only by our ruthless little predator.

"At least you didn't bring me a dead mouse this morning." I rub Mickles's chin. "Where's Tom?"

The cat, of course, doesn't answer. He doesn't stay either, and marches his fluffy butt off the bed and out the door.

Humidity from last night's storm still hangs in the air and the smooth cotton of my robe clings to my arms and hips. It's going to be a muggy drive to work today.

"Tom?" I duck my head out of the bedroom. The shower's not

running but the kitchen sink is—a low *clunk* echoes through the loft's pipes when Tom turns off the water.

Still barefoot, I pad down our short hallway, past the second bedroom and the bathroom, into Tom's studio area.

One of his huge canvases—it's at least five feet across and six feet high—leans against his easel facing away from me and toward the window. The morning light streams around its sides and the warm, red-hued reflections from the brick building across the street give it a halo.

I can't see what he started in the middle of the night, but it *glows*.

"How long have you been up?" I call as I tiptoe toward the painting. I don't know why I feel I need to be reverent. I see his paintings in production all the time. I'm usually posing for them. But this time, I just...

I don't know. I think I can feel it, whatever he's painting. It oozes through the canvas.

"I outlined it." Tom leans against the arch between his studio and the dining area holding a bowl of cereal, sock- and shirtless, his plaid sleep pants low on his hips.

He looks more at the canvas than at me, his expression the intense, piercing hardness he gets when his mind creates. I call it his "composition snarl" and it's damned sexy.

He's damned sexy standing there in nothing but his pajama bottoms and charcoal smudges. Three parallel marks run across the top of his left pec. He must have scratched an itch while drawing. Another smudge sits just under the leather cord around his neck, and a hint of green along his left shoulder. A dab of blue highlights the wonderful line of soft body hair running from his navel toward his groin.

"Take a look." He shovels a spoonful of crunchiness into his mouth.

I'd rather look at him, but I know marvels await on the other side of the canvas.

Several sketches lay on the floor at the base of the canvas, some of random plants, others of cityscapes. All with specific splashes of different colors.

Lines crisscross the canvas, some thick. Some thin. Little smudges of color dot open areas. Figures that might be human, might be... I'm not sure. Canid? Wolf or coyote, I think. They look haunting, but not in a werewolf kind of way. In a semi-surreal way.

"What is it?" I reach to touch what I think is a leaf, but pull back my hand. Tom doesn't like people touching his unfinished works.

"Bad dreams." He blinks a couple of times and his lips thin to a line, but he covers it by shoveling another spoonful of cereal into his mouth.

The dreams surface every so often. They did after his only-selling-two-paintings disappointment. I'm not surprised they surfaced last night, the way he reacted to Juri's presence at the concert.

Tom doesn't like to talk about his bad dreams; no matter how many times I ask, he deflects, usually with sex. I figure it's a moody artist thing—like his brothers, he has a good head on his shoulders. Better than me most of the time. He just needs a little relief.

Is sex instead of talking healthy? Unhealthy? I don't know. Am I selfish for wanting his touches more than I want to deal with him frowning? Probably.

I walk over, wiggling as I move, doing my best to work loose the belt of my robe with the movements of my hips.

Tom sets his cereal on the sideboard next to the arch. "I need to shower." He points at the blue smudge on his belly but he stares at my chest.

"We don't want to be late for work." I drop the robe onto the floor.

Tom palms both my breasts, one in each hand, and runs the pads of his thumbs over my nipples. "Sometimes I wonder if you're a dream."

He never says stuff like that. Never wispy, dreamy, idealizing words. He's more grounded than that. So the frown and the comment worry me.

His eyes look darker this morning, more pewter in the reddish glow of sunrise than their normal swirling, ocean-like blue-green, and they're bloodshot. His lids are puffy. The bad dreams did a number.

I press the full length of my naked body against his front. Let the grays and blues of dreams smudge onto me; I can deal with it.

If I've learned one thing from Tom, it's that I can allow him in—all of him, his dreams both good and bad, his smudges, his smile.

Tentatively, he brushes his big hands up my naked back. He strokes with his fingertips at the same time he presses his face against my hair. His breath glides over my ear and across my cheekbone, smelling more like the oats of his crunchy cereal than anything "morning"—or painterly.

The coolness of his skin surprises me. He's usually so much warmer than me, with his energy-consuming, muscular body, but working out here shirtless all night has left a chill in his bones.

He can't be this way. Not my Tom. The cold steals his charm and his wit; it takes away his ability to see in the world what needs to be seen. It closes him off and...

I press my face into his shoulder. I hold on for dear life. And I can't help but wonder if this time, I need to rescue him.

But from what? I don't know. He won't share his bad dreams.

"Is this about Juri Olson?" I ask. He'd been adamant last night about not being jealous and I was pretty sure he was more concerned about my emotions than his own. But it had all gone away quickly, and he'd enjoyed the concert.

Tom's hands cup my backside. He grips my flesh, his fingers kneading, and nibbles on my ear. His hard cock presses the flannel of his sleep pants against my belly. When he rubs, the cotton rubs with him, and a new heat scrapes across my skin. "Who?" he asks.

I shudder. Most of my worries dissolve into the friction of his body rubbing against mine, and I know that at least for the next few moments, neither of us will be worrying.

He lifts me off the floor and I immediately settle my legs around his waist. The flannel keeps us apart but does nothing to constrain his erection. He's perfect, my Tom. Strong in more ways than I can count.

A groping kiss lands on my chin, then another on my shoulder. He glances around as if unsure about how best to get the leverage he wants and the next thing I know my back thumps against the wall.

One hand lets go of my bottom while the other holds me in place. His bicep hardens as it presses into the side of my chest and I swear I almost come. Almost scream in ecstasy just from the feel of his muscles against my body.

Tom wiggles himself out of his sleep pants and slides the entire length of his cock against my slick clit. His mouth slants over mine. He inhales at the same time, forming a momentary vacuum.

All the tingles in my lower abdomen, all the electrical fire and the icy crackling, the small, fast shaking that vibrates my bones—they well upward into the vacuum caused by Tom's kiss. My chest shudders. My throat, my tongue, my entire mouth wants the texture and the slight saltiness of his skin.

His mouth lifts off mine and I gasp. Air rushes between us, over my lips, and cools the roof of my mouth.

He peers at my face as if taking in the totality of my expression at the same time he's examining each separate muscle pull, each blink, the depths of my pupils, the color of my cheeks. He knows the sum of me before he adds up my parts.

No man compares to Tom. No man has ever given me his complete focus. Or his strength. Or his hard desire.

Both of his hands grip my backside and he jostles me slightly to balance my thighs on his forearms, then pulls his chest off my body.

Come back, wisps through my mind and I almost say it. Almost whimper and pout because I can't stand *not* having him on me. I need his clean, masculine scent of paints and sandalwood. Life vanishes without his lips and his kisses.

Tom smirks as if he's read my mind. He spreads my legs wider, but only rubs the head of his cock against my clit this time. "You want that?" he growls. His grip on my thighs tightens and pressure almost to the point of pain fires up my legs.

Whatever triggered his new painting also triggered a roughness.

I usually don't like rough play. I don't like spanking or being held down. I don't like being tied up, either. It's not my thing, and it's never been Tom's thing. But right now, I think he needs a little rough release.

I bite at the skin over his collarbone.

His growl turns into an animalistic grunt. His pelvis shifts. Tom's brilliant, hard cock pushes deep into my pussy and it's almost too much. Almost more than I can take, the thrust, his strength, his size. He fills me perfectly, and he hits my deepest parts at exactly the perfect angle.

His next thrust slams me against the wall. When he pulls out, my body lifts up and cool air dances over my skin. My back arches. Tom growl-grunts again, and I'm flat against the wall, held there by the strength of his arms.

I bury my face against his breastbone. Sometimes he shaves his chest; sometimes he doesn't, and right now, a layer of soft dark hairs tickles my face and fills my nose with his scent.

The effort of holding me against the wall tightens his chest and shoulders. His upper body is as hard as his cock. His back tenses under my fingers.

I lose myself in the pounding wonder that is Tom.

His hands shift. He pulls me off the wall and spins me around until I land on the edge of his drafting table. He can't stay in me as my ass hits the smooth, glassy wood, and he's out. My body screams to get him back, to feel him filling me again.

His face reddens, as does his chest. I can tell he needs to be inside me as much as I need him.

I don't slide when Tom tries to adjust our position. The desktop grips my flesh and I lift myself up to reposition my bottom.

"Damn it." Tom picks me up. He's not going to wait for me to move on my own. He tosses me not-so-gently, and I land closer to the edge.

His mouth descends onto my nipple at the same time he thrusts in again. His entire body gropes, his lips and his hands. The roughness surfaces again and he pounds me fast—then stops. His cock jerks. Tom groans. His abs tighten and he first curls against me, then away, as his orgasm works around to his lower back.

"Sammie," he whispers. His muscles loosen, and his half-drunken, post-orgasm stupor makes his eyelids flutter.

I grab his hips and I swear the roughness travels from his skin, into my fingers, and up my arms. I want to come while he's fucking me; I want him to make me come.

Tom's eyes narrow. A new tightness makes him stand erect—he knows he's not done.

I love how he reads me, how he knows what needs doing. He pushes me down onto the table, but he doesn't pull out. I know how sensitive he is after an intense orgasm, how even the slightest touch to his cock can be too much, but he's fighting through it. Reveling in it, using the pain.

He slaps the pad of his thumb against my clit. Smacks me hard, then flicks with his pointer finger.

"Oh!" My hips roll involuntarily. I look up at the ceiling and my mouth opens.

"I have a new set of mock-ups I need to finish today." His words rumble from his throat.

Goddamn his voice is sexy. He could read the ingredient label off his cereal box and I'd come just from how he enunciates *syrup*.

He jitters his thumb as he presses into my clit. "You have memos to write."

Yes, yes, our work life is boring. "Every time I look at a memo from now on, I'm going to remember this."

"That's right," he says. "You will." He pinches my nipple.

My orgasm floods my entire body. I flop and twitch, and the table bounces. I know the boys downstairs—they come in around now—can hear me, but it only makes me hotter. Tom's not afraid to show the world what we have, and that's just fine with me.

He pulls out. He's off me with his sleep pants back where they should be before I sit up. A small smirk twists up one corner of his mouth before he kisses me deeply and pulls me to his chest.

"Did I banish the bad dreams?" I suspect I have—his body has returned to his smooth, loose warmth I'm used to—but I want to hear him say it, I think, more for him than for me.

"You make every morning better," he says. Then he's off to gather my robe from the floor.

But he's not smiling. He glances at his painting.

Right in front of me in the harsh, reflected morning light, I see the momentary banishment rescind. His lower back tightens first. The knot sets off a chain reaction up his spine and into the muscles between his shoulder blades. His neck stiffens.

Tom grins but his eyes look lost. He hands me my robe.

Then he walks away, toward the bathroom and his morning shower.

CHAPTER 5

Thomas

Sammie spent the drive to work watching me as if she expected my head to burst into flames. When she asked if I wanted to "talk about it" I told her the truth. I'm tired. That's all. Too much work and too little sleep. Just dreams.

My mood has nothing to do with Juri Olson.

Then she frowned and sighed and now I'm thinking I did something wrong.

She held my hand as we walked through the parking garage, the skyway, and into our building. She kissed me before making her way up the steps to her floor. But I think we might be heading for an argument.

I lean back in my clicking desk chair. The damned thing sticks when I turn or move and instead of gliding, it makes rattling *pop pop pops* that ping against my balls. It's not a sensation that helps anything, and my mood in particular.

Maybe I should talk to Dan. Ask if my adult-in-the-room older brother has general, overall adult advice. I hear his voice in my head already: "Why yes, young man, all us big boys worry about paying the mortgage." Not that he'd say it like that. The subtext would be there, though.

I rub my face. Manny, my boss, wants the new yogurt mock-up by the end of the day. It's an update, nothing major, just streamlining... more a test of graphic design than anything artistic.

I rub my face again. What is wrong with me? Why the fuck do I have a mortgage? I graduated a year ago. Shouldn't I be growing an ironic beard, living in a tent, and drawing the Grand Tetons because I'm young and unencumbered? Hell, my brother Rob took off with his girlfriend. They're in the wilds out west and he's only eighteen months younger than me.

Sammie is four years deeper into the whole adult thing. She wanted the loft. I want her. Seemed like a good trade-off.

A message pops up on my computer screen. Manny wants to talk to me in his office.

My stomach tightens. It shouldn't. He probably just wants to talk about the mock-up.

But that dream flickers into my mind—the sensation of drowning in a sea of biting, prehistoric plants juxtaposed on a human space, a concourse or mall or maybe a piazza, full of so many bodies I can't breathe.

I inhale. Close my eyes. Force my gut to calm. The dream flickers away just as fast as it butted into my head.

I walk across the open central area of the Art Department, past the two interns diligently filing or sorting or whatever it is that Manny sets the unpaid help to doing. Past my coworkers in their cubies. All the way to Manny's door.

I grip the frame. "You wanted to see me?"

Manny looks up from one of his screens. "Tom." He waves to the chair in front of his desk. "Sit down."

He's a squat little man, neither fat nor thin, with a rectangular build that makes him look like a brick with legs. His arms reflect his angles and long, straight lines, and even though they aren't stick-like, they lack muscular smoothness.

Manny, overall, gives off the impression of having been drawn by a five-year-old.

He's a passable artist. His skills come down more on the side of herding cats than drawing them, which is why he sits behind a big desk in a corner office. He's been with the company a solid ten years now, to my one.

Manny shuffles papers while I pull back the chair to give myself enough leg room. His office might be in the corner—he has a nice view of the skyscraper across the street—but it's not that large, and his desk and array of massive monitors take up most of it. We never have meetings in here, only one-on-ones.

I drop into the chair. Manny still isn't looking at me and my gut does another flip. The rumors must be true. They have to be true. Otherwise my boss would look me in the eye.

"Tom," Manny says again, but this time with a shallow, thin grin on his brick-like face. He's a bit ruddy as well, like a brick. I could toss him through the window and he'd fly all the way into the corporate banking offices across the way.

I *do* want to throw something. I want to break shit and yell *I just bought a loft, motherfucker!* But that won't help. Nothing ever helps in situations like this.

"Spit it out, Manny." What else can I say? Rip off that goddamned bandage, okay? Just rip it the fuck off and rub some dirt on it. Because that's what I'm supposed to do, right? Walk it the fuck off.

Manny sits back in his chair. "I want you to know that I was against this." He pushes a piece of paper toward me. "I know talent when I see it. I told HR to let me choose. I asked them not to deplete my talent pool, but that's not how the contracts work."

No, it's not. I've been on the outside of the herd since I started. It takes two years around here before they bring you into the center and protect you from the wolves.

Not that I would have had any more protection once I passed the two-year mark. The contracts are different now. The company isn't about to let go of the extra rope they reeled in during the recession, so vulnerable I am.

Sammie, though, should be okay.

Please let Sammie be okay, I think. We can't both get laid off at the same time. I don't want to sell the loft. I don't want to move back into my brother's basement.

I don't want Sammie to look at me and think that I'm not worth the time and effort she puts into me.

I pick up the piece of paper. Like all legalese, my layoff notice is in nine point font. It's blurry. HR needs a better printer.

A snort pops out before I can catch it.

Manny frowns. "Listen, kid, you're on the top of my list for re-hire, but don't hold your breath." He waves at the two giant monitors on his desk. "They give me that shit," he waves at the paper in my hand, "and with the other hand they tell me I'm now remotely supervising my new team." Now Manny rubs his face.

I feel bad for thinking about bricking him through the window, then I remember that I just got laid off, not him. I'm the one who will have to figure out how to pay for my new home. I'm the one whose fiancé might be getting laid off too, right now, in a different corner office on a different floor of the same soulless, colorless, shitty corporate building as me.

Why did I agree to buy that place when I knew I was vulnerable? Why did I think that the luck I'd had this past year—meeting Sammie, my gallery show, the opportunities—would hold? Shit like that never holds. Girlfriends meet princeling exes at concerts. Brothers spend months in a burn ward. Mothers die in car crashes.

Bubbles fucking burst.

"Oh, God." It pops out of my mouth and I fight the need to drop my head between my legs.

Manny sits there silent for a long moment, staring at my head. He blinks a few times, but his face stays the same flat cover-the-anger redness it's been since I walked into his office.

One of his monitors ticks like a fucking clock. *Tick click tick click tick tick tick* and I want to push it off his desk. I want to see it spark and snap broken on the floor in a pile because it should have known better than to think that its life would be smooth sailing the moment it accepted its Bachelors of Arts from the good school down the road.

I rub the top of my head, and sigh.

Manny drums his finger on his hollow desk. "I'll need your projects."

So much for finishing the mock-up. I nod.

He drums his finger again. "I know you're getting married soon."

"Yeah." We had a tentative date, but her family disagreed. Now we have "plans."

Plans that are likely to stay "plans" for quite a while, now.

"She's safe." A quick smile darted over Manny's face, then vanished again. "Do *not* tell anyone I checked, okay? I called in a favor." He hits his desk. "I wanted you to know. Seemed the decent human thing to do."

I push back my chair. I'm half tempted to leave the piece of paper on his desk, but this isn't Manny's fault. It's not HR's fault, either. Every person's responsibility within this multinational hive is as miniscule as they are. *I just print the pages. I just dot the 'i's. I just keep the company on the path the stockholders want.*

It's neither decent nor human.

My dream comes back to me—the mile-high, prehistoric palms, the oppressive humidity and air, the steep, disorienting climb.

Coyotes and wolves.

"I'll give you whatever recommendations you need, Tom." Manny's shuffling papers again. I suspect I'm not the only victim today.

"Thanks." I take the paper. I don't really have any other choice.

Time to clean out my desk.

CHAPTER 6

Samantha

He usually messages me at least twice during the afternoon. Small stuff like "thinking of you" or pictures of the little doodles he does when he's bored.

I got nothing today.

When it was time to go home, I went down to his floor early. A couple of his coworkers blinked open-mouthed as I walked by and quickly looked away. No one said hello.

Someone had cleared out Tom's cubie. Everything was gone—all his artwork, his comic book toys, even his trash can.

When I bumped into his cubie wall, his boss came out of his office. It took all my effort to not cry.

Where are you? I text. Why didn't he tell me? Why didn't he come upstairs and get me and let me help?

In the truck, he texts back. He went out to the parking garage?

I run from our building to the garage and up the stairs to the floor where we'd parked this morning. My bag thumps against my side and my pencil skirt constricts my legs, but I hit the hot, humid evening air less than five minutes after his message appeared on my phone.

My heart thumps from running but mostly it thumps from the thoughts spooling in my brain: Why didn't he talk to me? Is he okay? Will he do something stupid? Not Tom. He's the most level-headed man I know other than his brother, Dan. Should I call Dan or Tom's younger brother, Rob? Will we be okay? Will he find another job?

Maybe he won't.

"Tom?" I yell. We have options. We always have options. It's not the end of the world, so why am I yelling? The truck is parked around the corner and up the opposite side of the ramp, in neither sight nor hearing range of where I stand now. I shouldn't yell.

I hear an oncoming car but I run around the corner anyway, staying against the parked vehicles.

The guy comes so close he could have stuck his arm out of his window and hooked my waist. He glares at my face, then at my chest, before pushing up his sunglasses.

I stand there at the opposite end of the aisle from Tom's truck—from *him*—and my heart skips a beat. Right there, in my chest, it thumps, then doesn't, then thumps hard.

If I'm feeling like this, how is Tom handling it? I run the rest of the way to the truck.

He sits in the driver's seat, his head against the headrest. I can't tell with the shadows, but I think his eyes are closed. The windows are wide open, and his shoulders slump as if he's hanging one of his arms out, but otherwise, he doesn't move.

My gentle, together Tom is sitting alone in his truck in a parking garage full of assholes like the guy who just drove past me.

I walk around the back of the truck. Tom inherited it when Dan bought a new one a few years ago and it shows off Dan's firefighter history. Big and red, it looks official and important. But it's just our truck, and it takes us to work every day.

Or, now, just me.

Tom's big arm drapes out the window and he taps his index finger against the door handle. Even in his white button-down, his bicep pops. Finding athletic cut shirts big enough for his shoulders turned out to be a challenge; I'd started having his clothes tailored. I guess that stops now, as well.

"Tom?" I slide my hand from his elbow to his palm. Slowly, I wrap my fingers around his.

He sits up and opens his eyes. His gaze first drops to the mirror—he's looking at our hands—then he looks out at me.

When he sits in the truck, we're at eye level. I'm not short, but out of my heels and in my sneakers, my head tucks perfectly against his neck and my arms around his waist.

"I should have called you after my meeting with Manny." He closes his eyes again. "I'm sorry."

I glance into the space behind the seats. Three banker's boxes sit stacked against the back of the passenger seat, where Tom's little nephew Bart sits when he visits.

"Look at it this way, when you pull another all-nighter, you can sleep it off the next morning." It's stupid and it just pops out of my mouth.

Tom pulls in his arm. He frowns and looks away, obviously not charmed by my joke. "I'm still waiting to hear from that comic book editor." He taps the steering wheel. "She's going to tell me to work for a small company first." His frown deepens. "That's how they do it."

"Okay. Let's get you on a project." I'll need to research what's needed, and find the right people. There's a flourishing indie movement here. I could find him a writer. "I can do that. I'm your rep."

A deep furrow appears down the middle of his forehead. His lips thin, too, but his nostrils flare. "You have a real job."

I want to slap his shoulder. Right here, right now, with my heart thumpity-thumping and his ego shattering into tiny bits of male worthiness. I want to yell and roll my eyes and tell him he damned well better not be feeling sorry for himself.

But I don't think that would help.

"So do you." I pull the door handle and the latch releases.

Tom watches the door swing open. I step into the space between him and the metal panel, and toss my bag into the passenger seat. He frowns again as my stuff sails by his chest, but he keeps his eyes on me.

I don't know what he needs. I've never been laid off. So I wait.

He leans against the seat. Slowly, he rubs his face, but the frown stays. He closes his eyes again.

Somewhere nearby, a woman laughs. A car starts. The stink of exhaust mixes with the summer heat and humidity and does nothing to make either of us feel comfortable.

I can't wait any longer. "Hey..." I stroke his arm.

"I guess boring old me just became useless me, too, huh?" He continues to frown. The least he could do is smirk like his words are a terrible joke, but no, he continues to frown.

The desire to slap his shoulder surfaces again. "Are you seriously giving me that shit?" I hitch up my skirt and throw a leg over his lap. "I don't want to hear it."

He inhales as I wedge myself between his abdomen and the steering wheel. It's not comfortable. The wheel presses like a bar against my lower back and my skirt wads up between our bellies but I have his attention.

Tom smooths his hand up my outer thigh in the unconscious way he responds to my touches just before he realizes he's *responding*. His fingertips press yet a fraction harder as they flick over the lace topping my stockings. If he wanted, he could push that hand around and run his fingers over the smooth, soft black lace of my panties.

Sometimes I wear garters. Most days I pick out two or three pairs of itty bitty panties and a few pairs of thigh-highs and leave them on the bed while I shower. When I come out, Tom's made his choice.

Even with the sex, he didn't this morning. Now I frown.

But his big hand on my thigh is wonderful and mesmerizing and makes me feel better. I wiggle just enough to reinforce my distraction.

"What are you doing?" Yet he strokes my thigh again.

The door is wide open—or as wide open as it can get without denting the vehicle parked next to us. Tom glances over his shoulder at the garage as if a horde of disapproving old ladies is about to burst through the stairwell door.

I glance around, too. We're alone up here in the middle of the parking garage. "No one's around."

His frown turns into pinched lips. "Security cameras."

I throw my arms into the air. I'm straddling his lap with my skirt up around my waist and his big hand cupping my ass and he's frowning about security cameras?

"Sammie..."

I have no idea what he wants to say, nor do I understand why my attempt to cheer him up isn't working. "Are you going to pull a Dan on me?" His brother went into a full work-life balance freak-out with his now-fiancé Camille at the start of their relationship.

Sometimes the Quidell men retreat and fortify against a threat instead of meeting it head-on. I can't blame them, considering the pain they've lived through.

Tom pulls away from me. I'm wedged between him and the wheel and he still manages to back away from me.

"I have the right to ask, Tom." I'm *his* fiancé.

He closes his eyes again. "Can we go home? Talk about this in private?"

Slowly, I slide off his lap and back to the pavement, suddenly feeling overexposed. No one can see me—I'm between the truck's open door and the car next to us, completely surrounded by concrete and metal—but the disapproving look Tom throws me makes me feel small.

I smooth my skirt back where it's supposed to be.

"Hey." He drops his legs out the door, and pulls me close with one smooth motion. "I'm sorry." A kiss lands on my cheek. "It's not you."

But he sure just made me feel like it was me.

This time, instead of wiggling toward my hard, warm man, I wiggle away, between the cold metal of the truck's door and the vehicle parked next to it.

Tom watches me walk around the back of his truck to the passenger side, still frowning. Still with a shadow hanging over his blue-green eyes.

I crawl in and pull my seatbelt across my lap. "Let's go home."

CHAPTER 7

Thomas

I tap Sammie's note and it scrapes across the hard surface of our small kitchen table. She left it propped up against the salt shaker between a pile of paper napkins and a two-day-old pizza box. "Don't forget to eat," it says. Then "I took the bus," and "I love you."

She didn't wake me up this morning. She just left. Two weeks of me being an unemployed bum and she's leaving notes like I'm a latchkey kid.

I stare at my bowl of crispy dry cereal and my just as crispy phone. Reception's not good this morning and Dan's voice crackles through the speaker.

"I could use the help," my brother says. Like the good family man that he is, he called the moment my unemployed time passed the two-week mark. He decided he needed to tell me that his one-man company is hiring.

Which it's not. His buddy Jason has been helping out lately, so I know he's lying.

"And chance breaking my fingers?" I take a bite of my cereal. "How am I supposed to hand model with a splintered pinky?" I say around my oversweet manufactured morning food pellets.

"How would you break your pinky?" He sounds incredulous.

"I don't know shit about fire prevention, Dan." I don't. I'd just get under his feet the same way I did when we were kids.

I hear a sigh that signals a shrug. "That's not the point."

Of course that's not the point. But Dan's not going to come out and say the point any more than Sammie will. My brother offers me a pity job and my girlfriend leaves a pity note. They're both trying to spare my delicate artist's constitution.

I take another bite and stare at the note. Of course I'll eat. One can't face an email inbox full of editorial rejections on an empty stomach.

"It's only been two weeks." Closer to three, actually. I spend most of my time sending out résumés and posting portfolio applications. I think I've talked to every intern assisting the head intern who fetches coffee for every magazine, comic book publisher, and art editor in all the places where there are cities large enough to farm interns.

Sammie likes to tell me that "you have to do the leg work." So I do the leg work.

I take another bite of my cereal.

"I'm just saying that if you need work, there's work, okay?" I hear rustling on Dan's end. "Listen, I need to pick up Bart." My nephew is finishing up his summer program at the Community Center's daycare near where my brother lives.

Dan's fiancé, Camille, works there and usually brings Bart home. "Where's Camille?" I stuff the last pellets of cereal into my mouth and shove the bowl across the table before dusting crumbs off my t-shirt and sleep pants.

Maybe I should put on real clothes before Sammie gets home.

"She had a slight fever this morning." I hear Dan's truck start. "The 'no school if you're sick' rule applies to the teachers as much as it does to the students."

He sounds worried.

"Everything okay?"

Dan chuckles. "Rob called yesterday."

Robert, my dear invalid graduate student of a younger brother. "He's okay, isn't he?" He got hurt a few months back, but he seemed good when he left to explore the wilds of Colorado with his girlfriend, Isa.

"They got married."

"Married?" My little brother the player got *married?*

"Yep." I hear Dan's truck rumble. He must be pulling out of the lot.

"You're driving." We can talk about this later. I should text Rob and ask him why he didn't see fit to call both his brothers.

I frown at my phone as I pick it up off the table.

"Okay. Yeah." Dan's obviously no longer paying attention to me. "Think about it."

"I will." I end the call and I'm alone again with only my own sounds in the kitchen of my too-expensive loft.

Rob got married. I glance at the pile of dishes in the sink and the open cereal box on the table. Two baskets of laundry sit next to the washer. The studio needs vacuuming and I should change the sheets on the bed.

I toss my phone next to my laptop as I walk by the dining room table. Mickles looks up from his spot on his comfy chair and does his best *whatever, human* yawn. I walk on by, toward the only thing I know how to do—illustrate. Paint. Maybe make something salable.

I keep the cat fed and the art coming, so at least I have that going for me.

❧

SAMMIE LEANS OVER THE BACK OF MY CHAIR. IN FRONT OF US, ON MY computer's screen, my brother's wife leans toward her webcam and wiggles her wedding ring.

"Oh my God!" Sammie squeals right next to my ear.

She got home late. Didn't text me or anything, just dropped her bag at the top of the steps and pulled off her shoes so she could exchange war stories with Isa.

I do, though, get an "I'm sorry" hug when I cringe after the squeal.

Isa points at the camera. Her blonde hair's up in a messy knot-thing and she looks ghostly but happy. "Honey, set it on the table."

Rob grumbles something, and the view suddenly jostles.

Sammie kisses my ear. "We should set a new date."

We'd first thought a spring wedding, but her cousin's deployment meant she couldn't be a bridesmaid. Then Sammie and Camille started talking about a double wedding, but Sammie's mother threw a passive-aggressive fit. "Oh, sweetheart, you can do what you want," Lorna had said with an exaggerated crestfallen face. "But are you sure?" The lip had quivered. "It's *your* special day, you know."

There were arguments. I told her we should have eloped.

Now I'm unemployed. Or, as Sammie likes to say, a full-time artist.

Rob settles his phone and appears at Isa's side where she sits on their room's ridiculous bed. They're staying in some trashy, red and silver heart-themed hotel. "So," he says, all smiles, "I didn't tell Dan the big news when I talked to him."

Isa shakes her head *no*.

"You're pregnant!" Sammie blurts out.

Isa smiles and nods *yes*.

Sammie knocks my shoulder. "Bart's going to have a cousin."

Looks that way.

Sammie wags her finger at the screen. "After the way you two were going at it in the boat house at the lake, I bet you're carrying quadruplets."

Rob laughs, but looks embarrassed.

"It doesn't work that way, honey," I say.

Sammie gives me the side-eye. "It was a *joke*, Mister Mopey."

Rob's eyebrow arches. "How's the work coming? Any luck with that comic book editor?" He curls an arm around Isa.

"No word yet." Nothing. No word from any of the editors I've talked to.

"Oh!" Isa bounces a little. "I know a guy in L.A. who runs a story-boarding company. Do you want his name?"

"Yes," says Sammie, before I can answer. I frown.

"Okay." Isa grabs her phone off the table. "I'll message you."

The ladies talk and my brother and I stare at each other. He got married before me. Hell, at this rate, there's going to be Quidell babies everywhere and Sammie and I will still be engaged-with-no-date-set. Though, really, Dan is the only one of us financially ready to get married.

Sammie steps away to scroll through the info Isa's sending her.

"Have you talked to Dad recently?" A bit of worry mixes in with Rob's overall joyously stunned expression.

"Why?" I ask. "I talked to him the day we did the hand-off while you were an invalid after your incident." Rob got a knife to the gut. I flew out to help and stayed for as long as I could, but I had to fly home. Couldn't miss too much work. Dad flew in the same day. We ate lunch at the airport.

"He looked fine," I say. A little thin, but fine. Maybe more pale than a man living in Sedona, Arizona, should look, but I chalked that up to having a son knifed.

"Maybe you should go see him," Rob says. "It might be good for both of you."

Why would I do that? I think. Dad won't help. We'll talk about painting sunsets and mountain cactuses. He'll tell me not to worry about money even though it was his *not* worrying about money that caused so many of the fights my parents had. It caused all my mother's sixty-hour work weeks, too. Then he'll frown and be the Mister Mopey Sammie accuses me of being.

That's my dad, Jeremiah Quidell, the moody artist.

Rob must have read my expression because he pinches his lips. "He's proud of you, with the gallery show and everything."

I shrug.

I want to say "So?" but I'm not that much of an ass. Rob must have read that, too, because he shakes his head.

Rob watches Isa move around before leaning toward his phone. "What's gotten into you? You've been... angry... for a while now." He rubs at his stubble. "It started before you lost your job."

"I have no idea what you're talking about." The words drip off my lips.

Rob inhales. "I'm going to spend the next few weeks with my new wife before I fly back to school."

Isa ducks her head into the frame. "We're going to drive down to Sedona before heading to L.A." She drops onto the bed next to Rob and hugs his arm. "Come down! It'll be nice to see you again."

Rob gives me a *You heard the lady* look.

"Maybe after Tom gets work." Sammie scrolls through the information on her phone. She looks up. "A plane ticket right now isn't a good idea."

I look back at Rob and shrug once more. He nods and looks away, as does Isa.

They don't have any more money than we do, so why am I the one who feels like the little kid, here? But then again, I've been feeling smothered and treated like a child for a while.

Sammie grins and holds out her phone. "The storyboard company looks promising. Who knows, maybe we'll find a writer who wants to do a book with you."

I only nod.

Rob picks up his phone. "Time for food."

Isa waves. My brother cuts the call.

Sammie leans over my shoulder again. "A baby." She chuckles.

And for some stupid dumbass reason, my brain goes directly to imagining her thinking *Looks like you're now the irresponsible one.*

She leans against the table. "I could pull some funds out of savings." She points at the computer as if my family lived inside it. That's the Quidells, the brothers who lived in a shoe.

"If you do want to fly down to Sedona. You can read editor emails in Arizona as well as you can here."

I shake my head. "I don't want to see my father right now." I don't need the extra layer of his depressed shit he'd add to my life.

Sammie squeezes my arm. "I love you, ya know."

I pull her close for a hug. "I know," I say, and return to dredging the internet for illustration work.

CHAPTER 8

Samantha

A sliver of shimmering blue moonglow cuts between the curtains and over the bed, across Tom's back, and onto my breasts. A truck passes on the street below our loft, setting the window vibrating, and the slice of light wavers in unison with the big vehicle's rumble.

The flickers on me match the flickers on Tom, yet they don't.

He sighs and rolls under the stripe of moonlight so that his hip fully blocks the light from my body. Thomas Quidell, my big, wonderful man, takes the brunt of what pierces our life, even while he sleeps.

He's been cranky since we signed the papers for this place. Cranky about the renovations. Cranky about the costs. Cranky about the business side of his art career. Cranky about having to work a day job, and now cranky about *not*. I don't know what to do.

It's not like he won't get another job. He's smart. He's handsome. He's as hirable as they come. So I wonder if the crankiness is... something else. I wish he'd talk to me.

The low light of night turns our world gray. Mickles sleeps at the foot of the bed between my feet and Tom's, his fluffy buff fur a bright shadow. Tom's sandy hair looks almost gunmetal. The dark blue of our sheets has turned black.

If only the world was so simple.

I miss Tom the way he was when we first met. I miss his smile and his wide-eyed yet rock-solid belief in the certainties of life—that hard work would get him where he wanted to be. That his talent was enough. That I could—and would—be the good woman he needed.

I close my eyes and wonder why it is that I don't just go to sleep and leave the fretting to the cat. But if I learned one thing from Tom it's that letting bad—unhappy or cranky or whatever—feelings simmer only leads to all sorts of bad results.

He sighs again, and his arm moves under the blanket. Muffled mumbles vibrate into his pillow. He's not sleeping soundly.

That, I can help with.

Slowly, I wiggle toward Tom. Mickles *merps* displeasure as I maneuver my toes around his unmoving cat body. Tom sighs again, and more mumbles follow.

He rolls onto his side, and directly into me.

The blanket lifts ever so slightly as his hand lands on my hip. His wonderful, natural, male heat cascades over my body and for the first time since this afternoon, my muscles loosen. Tom—even a stressed-out, cranky Tom—makes the world livable.

"*Ummm...*" I nuzzle in close and rub against his front as I fold my arm around his waist. We're naked and chest-to-chest with each other in the moist summer air. No human noises seep in from outside—no more trucks or people laughing as they walk by on the sidewalk below. No flickering lights from the restaurants down the way. Nothing but us.

I press my face against his neck and inhale all the way to the base of my lungs.

Tom's mumbles turn into throaty words. "You okay?" He lifts his hand off my hip and rubs his eyes. "Can't sleep?" The hand returns to my shoulder. Gently, he runs his fingers up and down my arm.

I kiss the underside of his chin.

Tom chuckles. His hands move to my waist and he carries me with him as he rolls onto his back.

He has the most perfect, masculine hands—huge and sensitive, and not quite clean. He always has a fleck of some color embedded in the skin of his fingers, no matter how he scrubs and keeps himself tidy. I think it irritates him but I find it intriguingly sexy. He carries the proof of his talent and his hard work with him everywhere he goes.

He grips my hipbones with delicate precision, but he slowly blinks and wiggles his nose as if he's about to fall asleep again. "And here I thought I was the one who was supposed to wake you up for sex."

"If you lived with you, you'd be waking yourself up for sex all the time, too."

He chuckles again. "I must be dreaming. That almost made sense." His hands move up and he pushes me to sitting. I straddle his hips and wiggle, to keep his hardening cock against my folds, and rub my breasts.

Tom watches with hooded eyes, his face a flat sort of half-asleep impassiveness that looks neither real nor dreamlike. Maybe I shouldn't have woken him up. Maybe I should have let him sleep. Shame on me for thinking a little intimacy would do him good.

He twists his head to the side as he watches me. He takes over massaging my breasts, one big hand on each; he alternates flicking one nipple, then the other, then the first again.

The rhythm feels off, and too fast, as if he has no sense of his own heartbeat, or mine. As if he's not really thinking about what he's doing.

"If you don't want to, we can—"

He sits up and flips me around before I can finish my thought. I flop onto the mattress under him, my legs still around his waist. He moans against my neck, but his lips don't explore. He nips instead.

"I was dreaming," he says, his words sounding as if he's speaking around pebbles.

"About what?" God, the nipping and licking he does along my neck feels *brilliant*. I dig my nails into the flesh of his backside and press the full length of his erection against my belly.

He mumbles something I don't understand and his face vanishes from my neck. He lifts off me and cold air suddenly fills the vacuum he leaves behind. My back arches and a light, surprised gasp leaves my parted lips. The sheet flutters around us, rustling and wavering.

Tom's hand splays over my breast. He maneuvers his fingers until he has my nipple between his thumb and forefinger. He pinches. Hard.

I gasp again, but this time, his other hand cups under my ass—and just as the sheet settles, just as the shudder moving from my chest out to my limbs reverberates back up into my belly—Tom's mouth descends onto my pussy.

No slow, teasing kisses. No build up. He presses in the tip of his tongue and the not quite right rhythm flicks across my clit.

Yet his tongue accomplishes its goal. I stutter-gasp as my entire body responds to the oddness of Tom's groggy, groping touches. I wiggle and rub against his mouth. He grasps my hips and pushes me down into the shadows under the sheets.

I'm sucked into the not-quite-right world of the rhythm. The place that makes Tom jumpy and... cranky. There's no focus here and it's a little scary.

My adrenaline crests. Tom's form under the sheet outlines against the gray of the night. He traces his tongue along my clit and I can't take much more. I can't handle the overwhelming stimuli flooding my senses.

Tom sucks my clit between his lips at the same time he presses with the tip of his tongue.

My orgasm explodes from my core out into every cell of my body. A loud moan rolls from the base of my lungs. I grip the sheets.

The bed groans. Tom's off me again and the sheets flutter, flooding my skin, once again, with cool air. I blink, trying to focus, trying to see what he's doing, but he's under the sheet, hiding in there, in the dark, between my legs.

He yanks me toward him. I slide up his thighs and the head of his cock presses into me. A growl rolls from his dark place under the sheet. He moves my legs higher along his sides at the same time he leans forward.

He slides in deep. One hand lands next to my shoulder to support his weight while the other curls around my hip to hold me where he wants me.

The sheet hides his face, but it does nothing to impede his fast thrusting. The bed bangs against the wall with each hit and jolts me back toward him.

"T..." The next thrust rips through my body. "Tom..." And the next. He doesn't stop. "What?"

I wonder if he's fully awake. I wonder if he's still inside the dream he didn't tell me about. If...

I sit up and knock the sheet off his head and shoulders. Damn it, I want to see his face. He doesn't need to stay in the shadows.

He drops on top of me and buries his face against my shoulder before I can discern the look in his eyes or the set of his lips. The pounding continues with the same not-quite-right rhythm and the same, not-quite-good dreaminess.

His breaths shift to ragged. His chest tightens, as does his core. Tom slams into me one last time as his cock twitches inside me.

His weight presses me into the mattress. He mumbles something again, something I cannot understand, and rolls enough his head hits the pillow.

"Tom?" I whisper, but his arm over my hip loosens. He's asleep again.

I want to stay next to him. I want to cuddle against his broad chest and feel the soft hairs over his heart tickle my lips. I want to feel his grin against my temple and his breath against my hair. But he's been through a lot. He needs his rest.

I roll back to the cold shadows of my side of the bed.

CHAPTER 9

Samantha

I stare at the word salad of a memo on my computer screen. New interdepartmental communications "best practices" just came down from the overpriced consultants the big bosses brought in six months ago. Most of it is standard Communications 101 bullshit—clear language, bullet points—and the rest reads like a Jenga tower of jargon.

I've been fighting a headache all morning. The pain started when I tripped over Mickles in the dark hallway on the way to the bathroom. I'd left the lights off so as not to wake Tom. Then my bus was late. Now I have to look at meaningless razzle dazzle spewed by consultants who are all show and no substance. I have to hand it to them, though: They swoop in, do nothing but talk fast, then produce a report and a slick video and *boom!* all the company's ills are magically cured. They get paid and my fiancé gets laid off.

I lean back against the nylon weave of my desk chair, tip up my chin, and close my eyes. I used to like my job—maybe not so much "liked," but tolerated well. It was diverse enough to keep me from getting too bored. But I don't know anymore.

The work is pushing me away. *Tom* is pushing me away, even as I try to give him the space he needs. And I don't know what to do.

Maybe I should be the one looking for a new job. Something that pays better, so I can support him while he becomes established.

I wish I knew what to do.

The wall of my cubie rattles. Andy leans against the edge of my cubicle's padded wall, one arm over the top and the hand of the other holding a coffee mug. A pair of reading glasses sits on his perfect, straight nose. He wears a well-tailored, bright white dress shirt today, one that looks managerial except for its obvious quality, and a tie that probably cost more than Tom's truck.

Andy, my buddy and the best work husband a girl can have. He's also the source of much of Tom's early art career success.

On the surface, Andy is Juri Olson, but younger—beautiful, brilliant, and American royalty. He comes from money—a lot of money, to be honest—and doesn't need to work here, yet he does. It's his life, he likes to say, and he owns it. He'll wear what he wants to wear and he'll work the job he wants to work. He wants to live like a normal human being.

Andy didn't go into the family tech business, nor did he decide to make more wealth from his family's already vast wealth. I think the whole cutthroat world of the super-rich makes him uncomfortable.

He's way too smart and way too handsome to be a "normal human being" no matter what he says. I often wonder if there's something else going on in his life he doesn't want to talk about, but I won't pry. It's not like he's shy about asking my opinion. When he wants it, he asks.

His expertly-cut, chocolate-brown hair looks a little shaggier than usual today, and he has hints of darkness under his blue eyes, which must be the reason for the coffee.

He sniffs and pushes his glasses up his nose. Not that he really needs the glasses, either, but he's taken to them recently.

"So," he says with a totally straight face, "if you could go ahead and not mope, that'd be great."

I cough out a snicker. I can't be too loud or one of the idiot consultants might point out that I'm not jargoning my bullet points well enough, and then I'll get laid off, too.

The snicker turns into a snort before it's completely out.

Andy stands up straight. "Tom find new work yet?" He quickly glances around our office floor before walking into my cubie and dropping into my guest chair.

I shake my head *no*.

He sets his mug on my desk and leans forward. "Maybe you should take a few days off. Take Tom up to that lake place his family has." He nods northward.

I point at my computer screen. "Probably not a good idea to take a vacation right now."

Andy sits back in the chair. It groans—the furniture in the cubies isn't quality—and laces his hands behind his head. "How's the repping business coming along?"

It was Andy's ties that got Tom his first big art sale, and the gallery space. Without his help, I would be "repping" Tom with zero leads.

I shrug. "He's sending out résumés. Calling editors. He's looking for illustrating work right now." Stuff to pay the bills. "He started a new painting the morning he got laid off."

He's done nothing with it for three weeks. I haven't asked him about it—I usually don't and let him work in peace—but this one looks different from his usual work. I'm not in it, and the "people" inhabiting the landscape are more metaphorical than figurative.

"It's dream-like," I say. "The palette is different from his usual colors." I wish he'd go back to working on it.

Andy picks up his coffee cup. "He needs a commission."

"Like what? I've been pulling every competition and call I find." Public art, private art—I've been doing my legwork, too.

Andy stands and shrugs. "How about a casino? They rotate art through those places." He winks. "Makes them classy."

At the concert, Juri said something about the Olson Companies buying up properties in Nevada—a hotel on the Strip and another resort—and that he was scouting new talent.

Juri has an interest in fine art—not an in-depth interest by any means, but he does have an intrinsic ability to read what is in front of him. He's the same with people, both friend and foe. Juri knows how to read the signs, so Juri knows how to play the game. I once saw him read the waitstaff of a restaurant and use their enthusiasm or lack thereof to manipulate a takeover bid.

Juri understands cutthroat.

He was probably doing the same thing at the concert. Reading the intensity of the band's fans. Gauging the opinions of the venue staff. Making the correct plan to use the art made by a group of college kids to leverage himself a multi-million-dollar entertainment business.

Because that's what it is with Juri. Business.

Could I get Tom a slice of that multi-million-dollar pie?

Andy pats my shoulder. "It'll happen." Then he points at my screen and says, "Nose back to the grindstone, whelp."

No matter how I want to dive into a Juri-defined rabbit hole to chase after some sparkly maybes, someone needs to keep the job with the health insurance. Andy takes his coffee and his reading glasses, and returns to his corner of our grindstone, leaving me to stare at the consultant-tossed word salad. I stare. I try. I do. But I keep thinking about the hotel lobbies in Las Vegas.

And about Juri Olson. Do I call him? Tell him I'm repping my painter fiancé and my photographer sister-in-law?

I'm sure Juri has better things to do than help out a woman he dated five years ago.

I do a little Juri Olson internet stalking anyway. Turns out he still lives in the massive lake house on the west side of town, still holding down the local end of his father's business. His company's website touts "extensive growth" over the past three years, including a foray into finance and a new deal as major stockholders of the big resort hotel chain he mentioned at the concert.

Juri grins out from my computer screen, his warm, slightly orange-ish-brown eyes piercing and mildly predatory. His blue-black hair sits short and well-trimmed against his scalp, a tight cap of coolness on his compact build.

In the photo, he stands with another man in front of an expensive-looking reception desk, his feet apart and his hand coming in for a dominant handshake.

The photo screams "Juri Olson, man in charge."

Juri might just be the ticket I need. Not just for Tom, but perhaps for Dan's company, too. Tom's brother does a lot of work with hotels with fire safety and making sure they're up to code.

I look at my phone, then back at my screen, then to my phone again. Do I call his office? Send him a text? Fill out the online contact form?

Do I go home and talk to Tom about it first? I'm pretty sure he won't be happy about me talking to my ex.

I feel my lips pucker. I don't have to clear my activities with my fiancé. I'm doing it to help him, not hurt him, anyway.

I pick up my phone and dial Juri's office.

A receptionist answers. "Olson Companies."

"Hi," I say. How do I phrase this? I'm one of Juri's many exes and I'm looking for a favor? "My name is Samantha Singleton. I met Mr. Olson—Juri—at a concert about a month ago." I chuckle, mostly for show. "I hadn't seen him in years!"

That should get me past the front desk filter.

The receptionist doesn't say anything.

"Anyway," I say, "Juri mentioned that he was there to scout the band for the company's new venue holdings." It's a leap because that's not what Juri said, but I don't believe for a second he was scouting a young band just for the Vegas hotels.

And it dawns on me—Juri and his company are looking for a way to make his hotels a destination for younger people. He needs music. Media. He needs vibrancy.

"Yes..." says the receptionist. She's danced this dance before. I'm losing her.

"All the time I've known Juri, the concert was the first time I've seen him having fun while scouting." Am I lying? Probably. Still, it's a cutthroat world.

The receptionist chuckles. "We told him that Barston Flood wasn't a band who would cooperate with corporatism. He's still holding out hope."

"My thoughts exactly." I chuckle, too. "I was thinking about what he's been trying to do with the bands and the destinations and everything."

I hope I'm correct about my assumptions. If I'm not, I just blew it big time.

"I thought I'd let him know that I'm now repping an up-and-coming painter and illustrator. I'm also repping a spectacularly talented photographer. They're both young. Both intense and vibrant."

I pause. "It's not just bands people want to see. They want the whole experience."

The receptionist makes an affirmative sound. "Why don't you give me your information. I'll pass it on to Mr. Olson's assistant."

"Barb?" I ask, my fingers crossed. I met Barb once. She smiled and went on about her business ignoring Juri's girlfriend. But name dropping will likely actually get my info to Barb—and to Juri.

"Yes, Barb."

My finger taps my desk without me realizing that I'm fidgeting. I look down at it and purposefully force my hand to relax.

I give the receptionist my info. We chat a little about Barston Flood's fiery lead singer and our mutual love of good music. Then I say thanks and set my phone on my desk.

Why am I shaking? This is my job. My dream job, to be honest, representing talent so that they don't have to deal with the throat-cutting of the corporate world.

If I can get a commission for Tom out of this, seeing Juri again and dealing with his mega-corp will be worth it.

I return my attention to the consultant-generated salad of letters and numbers on my computer screen. Someone needs to keep the health insurance active.

I tap away at my keys, hoping that maybe, just maybe, Tom and I can finally move beyond bullet points.

CHAPTER 10

Thomas

I tap at my laptop and stare at my online résumé. My pasta and meat sauce dinner—leftovers from Saturday's night out with Sammie—sits cold and heavy next to my elbow.

Our big dining room table—the one her parents brought down from Grand Forks—spreads out before me. The one with sketches and Sammie's notebooks and folder full of gallery cards and business info. The table was meant for entertaining. Now it's just another desk.

I guess we won't be having any guests or parties with me moping around unemployed.

I take a sip of my summer craft beer from a random local brewery. Sammie figured since we bought a loft in a trendier part of town, we should be drinking trendy beer, too.

Trendy, expensive beer in a trendy, expensive loft purchased on the promise of two consistent incomes.

I sit back and look up at the rough-hewn ceiling above my dining room. I got that job pretty much the moment I graduated from the University. I met Sammie a few weeks after starting. My life looked bright and brilliant and now I'm wondering if I can handle being an adult.

Dishes rattle in the kitchen. "I think you should add a picture of the wall to your online portfolio," Sammie calls. The sink faucet starts up, then stops. "The design you did over the arch between the dining room and your studio. It shows your range of mediums."

Different orange tones and textures sweep across the wall. I did it for Sammie—clear tones of orange make her happy—but I don't want people thinking I will faux paint an Italian fresco on their suburban bathroom walls.

She ducks her head out of the kitchen. "Please."

I don't know who the fuck she's going to show my portfolio to that she hasn't already. Interior designers? What sort of hell would that be?

"Why?" I ask.

My thoughts must have been all over my face because her lip quivers just enough I see it from my spot at the table. She looks away and backs into the kitchen again.

"Because I made a call today," she says. "One that might lead to a commission. It'll help for them to see your full range."

I'm up and standing in the doorway to the kitchen before she's toweled off the plate in her hand. "Who did you call?"

She sets down the plate. "You need to stop feeling sorry for yourself."

"I just got laid off!" I want to slap the wall but I'm not a kid. I frown instead.

Sammie frowns right back at me and picks up another plate.

She didn't answer. "Who'd you call?" I ask again.

She inhales deeply and her breasts thrust out. Like all nights, she was out of her work clothes, make-up free, braless, and in her sweats within minutes of climbing the steps to our second floor loft.

Usually, seeing her fresh and free makes me happy. I like being the man who sees all of her facets. It's meditative, watching her transition from heels and corporate to home wear.

Today, I didn't pay attention when it happened.

All her air whistles out her nose. "Your plan was always to paint, Tom, remember? To make a living as an artist."

The problem here isn't the painting part, it's the making a living part.

She sets the towel on the counter and pads over to me. My lovely Sammie, my muse, looks up at me with her perfect eyes. She's the free spirit. All the good in my world wrapped up in auburn hair, hazel irises, and a soft, sensuous body that makes me happy to be alive.

"Don't lose yourself in losing something you never wanted in the first place."

What *do* I want? I watched Dan's life fall apart after his injury. I moved into his house to help with Bart.

When I was a kid, my mother worked a corporate job and, in what little time she had between mothering four kids, managed my father's art career. Then she and my sister died in an accident and my dad's life died with them.

I don't know why I'm thinking about the crash. I don't know why I'm thinking about Dan's injuries, either. I'm not wounded. At least not physically.

"Do you still want to marry me?" I just blurt it out. The question pushed out my mouth from some part of my brain that usually gets filtered by the parts that think things through. Except this time, they didn't catch the thought. They didn't yell, "Whoa, there, young man. Let's think about this for a moment, shall we?"

Nope, that didn't happen.

Sammie looks shocked. Not fake shocked because she should look shocked at such a question, but genuinely shocked and... frightened.

I scared my fiancé.

"Why would you ask me that question?" She hasn't moved. She stands perfectly still next to the sink in her sweats and her socks with the color draining from her face.

I don't know why I asked. I don't know why I'm standing here in the door between the dining room and the kitchen feeling as if the loft I share with the woman I love is imploding around me. The building is condensing into a black hole and I'm about to get sucked over the event horizon.

Sammie grips the towel. "Do you want to marry *me*?"

"Yes." Only an idiot would say no to Sammie.

She doesn't look like she believes me. She looks down at her feet for a long second, then inhales again. When she looks up at me, she smiles. "We'll get it worked out. Don't worry."

Don't worry, I think. *Don't fucking worry*.

I glance over my shoulder at the arch and its layers of color. On this side, it's a honeyed blue. I close my eyes and the afterimage turns an odd, artificial yellow.

It's easy for me to get lost in colors and paint strokes. In arches and circles and the laying down of meaning. It'll eat my life, if I let it.

I turn my gaze back to Sammie. Which part of my life is eating away at her?

I wish I knew.

I wave my hand in a wide sweep, and do my best to grin because I'm not supposed to *fucking worry*. "I'll take pictures."

Sammie's trying to not worry, and damn it, I can try, too. I turn around—more, I think, so that she can't see my face than because I don't want to walk into the wall—and stride purposefully through the arch.

My camera sits on top of a small cabinet next to the window. I keep most of my supplies in the shadows near the stairs down to our front door but I like to have a few things close.

I snatch up the camera. The arch glows golden at about ten in the morning. The light's angle coming in through our big window pulls the depths of paint layers to the surface. Maybe I should wait until the morning.

But Sammie wants photos now, so photos I will take. I snap one, but it's dark. "Picture looks terrible," I yell.

Sammie, a plate and towel in hand, walks around the table. Slowly, she runs her fingers over the raised edges of the arch's painted swirls.

Her smile's gone. "Would fill lights help?" Her face takes on a flatness I don't like. "In case J... they look at your portfolio tonight."

The pause makes my back stiffen, not so much because it existed, but because of how she rounded her lips just before she was about to make a "J" sound.

My grip on the camera tightens.

A streak of light fans out from our wide window, first touching my arm before sliding along the bamboo floor to Sammie's toes. A corresponding rumble shakes the entire building, starting near Sammie, then moving toward me.

The light and the sound, they're going in opposite directions.

"Did you call Juri Olson?" She called her *ex*. The super-rich guy old enough to be my father. The guy whose family owns one of the ten largest corporations in the state. "Why?"

Sammie's eyes widen. "Because you need a commission. Juri's working on upgrades to a major hotel and resort chain. I think he's trying to build a destination ethos that appeals to young people. He needs good art. Items that resonate with people our age. Things that speak to what our generation wants."

I close my eyes. "You sound like a goddamned brochure."

When I open them again, she's looking down at the plate in her hand. "I did what you wanted me to do! I made a connection. You could come out of this a millionaire. Imagine if the Olson Companies wants to make a big deal about unveiling your art. They operate with multi-million-dollar advertising budgets! All of a sudden, you're the guy everyone wants."

And I'll be doing TED talks about how wonderful my sell-out life is, I think.

Sammie sets the plate onto the sideboard next to the arch. Slowly, she wipes her hands on the towel. "It's like a gallery show, but bigger."

"No, it's not." I lean against the frame of the window. A bus rumbles down the street toward our building—it's one of the big new ones with the electrical motor kit sitting on top like a big spoiler. "They'll want corporate art."

"And illustrating comic books isn't corporate?" She crosses her arms over her chest. "Last month, you were drawing *corporate* yogurt and *corporate* cereal cartoon characters."

"That's not art."

The bus rolls close enough I see the advertisement along its side.

Yogurt. Goddamned, frankenfood, corporate yogurt using an illustration I did last year for the company.

My illustration. My work-for-hire, pay-the-*fucking*-bills drawing of happy GMO yogurt is on the side of a goddamned bus for the whole fucking world to see and they *laid me off*.

Sammie sighs and looks up at the ceiling. "Maybe Rob's right. Maybe you should visit your dad. Might do you good." She walks into the dining room and starts fiddling with the mess on the table. "Maybe you'll listen to another artist."

"My dad never sold out." Not until after Mom died. Not until he had to. Dad never drew fucking yogurt.

The bus rolls away, but I don't look at Sammie. I watch corporate America pass me by.

"What does 'selling out' even mean, Tom? Or commercial? Or corporate?" She slaps her towel against the sideboard.

I fiddle with the camera strap. "Gallery shows are about art. The cereal boxes were work-for-hire." And getting laid off.

Fucking predatory vultures.

She frowns and looks away. "I can keep a rein on the contracts, Tom. I can keep the corporate part of any offer from the Olson Companies from interfering with your art."

I look over at her. She stands with her hands on her hips and her face in her pinched, hard mask of anger. At least she's no longer scared or annoyed. Anger is easier to deal with.

Except my own. Does she want to handle Juri Olson on her own, without me around to interfere?

Alone. Without me. To interfere.

"I can't think about this right now." I set down the camera and stomp away from the window, toward the other side of my studio.

The dream painting, the one with the concourse and the primordial plants and the wolf-coyote-human hybrids and the emotions is right there leaning up against the wall, mocking me. *Get your shit together*, it's saying. *Figure it out.*

And all I can think about is the psychobabble Dan's therapists like to tell him: Be true to your authentic self. Take concrete steps. Understand the moment and the context of a let-down and don't generalize to the whole wide fucking world.

For a second, I wonder if my authentic self is lost somewhere inside that painting. If that's why I stopped working on it after I got laid off. If I put *me* in there, Dorian Gray-style. Except I don't think the painting will reveal the corruption of my soul. I think I can do that all on my own.

Behind me, Sammie is now slapping papers and folders and cups against the table top. In front of me, my "art" rolls its eyes and gives me the finger.

Comic books. Cereal box cartoon characters. Storyboards. A rich man's whims.

And art.

I slip my feet into my shoes. I'm down the stairs to the street and out the door before Sammie calls my name.

I just need time to think, that's all.

CHAPTER 11

Samantha

The bus bounces along toward downtown and my office job. I, once again, left this morning before Tom woke up. He's been sleeping later and later. And now he's pissed at me for trying to help.

He came back to the loft about an hour after he went out walking, then frowned and gave me a hug before walking into his studio without another word. He was still out there when I went to bed.

I checked this morning. He didn't start a new project last night. Nor did he work on the big painting. I don't know what he did.

I watch out the bus window, turned so that I don't have to interact with the kid sitting next to me. Lanky, dark hair, ironic beard scruff— he looks young and is probably on his way to the University. Smells good, too, which is a nice change of pace for the bus. I think he dropped into the seat for the same reason a lot of men like to sit next to me.

I don't want to chat or be friendly, so I do my best to keep my back to the poor guy. He compensates by being young and staring at his phone.

60

He's Juri's target market. The serious young person looking to make his own mark on the world. To buy his own brand of car and his own new model of smartphone. The group, I think, Juri Olson wants to hook with a vacation, spa, self-care destination all their own.

Why is that bad? Why is talking to the kids like they are adults a bad thing? God knows they get more than their share of stupid nostalgia thrown at them. I think they buy it not because they want to watch the same cartoon princesses they watched when they were ten but because no one's come up with anything new to offer.

I could be wrong. I could be right. I'm twenty-eight. It's not like I'm an old lady.

It's not like Tom's a kid, either.

Why can't we be part of the adulting that the corporate world offers?

Tom just needs someone who understands that corner of the world to explain it to him. Someone with a view of the whole project.

The guy next to me slides his thumbs across his phone's screen. Outside the bus, traffic swirls and upset drivers glare up at us passengers as they accelerate on by. One guy looks at whatever ad is on the side of the bus—I don't know, I didn't look before I got on—then scowls at me like I'm the root of all advertising evil.

Maybe I am. Maybe the ad on the bus is some engineered food product perfected by the mad scientists in research and development at my frankenfood corporation and the guy in the car knows just how bad that shit is.

I sit back in my seat. The cute college boy next to me grins. I realize that I can't be confined by Tom's mood, or by the list of editors to whom he's sent résumés. Or, for that matter, by waiting for Juri's assistant to call.

I grin back at the kid as I pull my phone from my pocket.

I don't keep my exes' numbers on my phone. I do, though, keep them, along with contact information and email addresses, in a folder in one of my online profiles.

Some of my exes are good guys. Some are total douchebags. Some, like Juri, might just be valuable as a future contact.

I log on and swipe through my archived contacts. And there it is, the personal phone number for one Mr. Juri Olson.

He probably changed his number. It's been five years. I'll probably get a college kid like the guy sitting next to me.

But I won't know until I try. I copy his number into my dialer. The call goes to voicemail and a generic "Leave a message" recording.

It's Juri's voice and the same greeting he used when we dated.

"Juri," I say. "It's Sam." I use Sam and not Sammie. Or Samantha. Best to give Juri an offering. "I was wondering if your receptionist passed on my message." I pause again. "Text me or give me a call if you're interested."

Leave it open-ended. Get him hooked. See what happens.

I disconnect wondering if I'm being icky. What if he calls looking for a blowjob? But Juri's not an asshole. He's just driven. And arrogant. And a bit of an egomaniac.

Even if Juri was listening to my message right now, he won't call back until this afternoon. He never immediately calls anyone back. Not his girlfriends. Not his father. Not even his own daughter.

Guess I'll have my answer when I have it. I tuck my phone into my pocket and return to looking out the window.

And all I can think is, *this better work*.

🙚🙘

SUN STREAMS IN FROM THE TRANSOM OVER OUR DOOR—IT'S FULLY sealed and we can't open it, no matter how handy that might be—but it does add a bright flare of light to what is a narrow, dark passage. Tom had made a few offhand comments about painting what is basically our front walk, but he hasn't done it yet.

I drop my bag on the floor at the top of the stairs. He can paint it later, after he feels settled again. I'm hoping Juri's text will help.

A simple *Let's meet* came in late in the day just as I was walking out to the bus stop. I texted back that I would call his receptionist tomorrow morning, so now's the time to get Tom excited and willing to smile at the man who might be funding his career for the next decade.

I need to text Isa. Let her know that I'm about to set up a meeting that might land her work, as well.

My shoes follow my bag as I look around. Tom isn't in his studio. I glance at the kitchen. The light is off. I glance down the hall. The bedroom light is off, too.

"Tom!" Did he run off again? I walk into the dining room. Maybe he left a note.

Nothing. I walk back out to the studio. Nothing there, either. His space smells dusty. Dry. Not full of the slightly tangy scent of his oil paints, or the slightly damp smell of his watercolors. I don't inhale the grit of pencils, either.

He's not just hiding his work, he's not producing.

The giant, stalled painting still leans against the wall and I swear it has a dullness to it as if Tom's neglect has made it lonely.

I run my finger over the smooth wood of his easel. It's a massive, solid thing, built with love by Tom and Dan. They even sanded it smooth and applied a coat of lacquer. It's smothered in color now, blues and reds and burnt siennas. All the colors Tom uses when he paints portraits of me.

I haven't sat for him since he started the huge painting. I haven't sat for him since he lost his job. He hasn't asked. I haven't offered. We've been busy.

I look up at the ceiling. How do I feel about Tom's nudes of me filling the galleries of a major hotel chain? About kids like the guy on the bus this morning looking at all my parts?

The thing is, they won't be looking at me. They'll be looking at Tom's expression of aspects of me. Parts he sees. Parts that never change. Parts I'm not even sure I understand myself.

His paintings are more a reflection of him than they are of his subjects.

Mickles meows somewhere down the hall, and I hear shuffling.

It's almost dinner time and Tom's still sleeping? No wonder he hasn't been working.

Mickles trots down the hall and directly to my ankles. He meows again and does a leaping full-body rub complete with wrapping his soft, fluffy tail around my leg.

At least the kitty wants to see me.

Tom walks into the open area between the stairs and his studio. He stops and blinks, then rubs his messy sandy-brown hair. "What time is it?"

I don't think he's taken a shower today. I know he hasn't worked out in about a week. He says he's fine but I know running and lifting help him stay stable.

Not that he'll listen to me.

"Dinner time."

He blinks again and points at the kitchen. "What do you want?" Now his other hand lands on his head. "I haven't cleaned up the dishes yet."

"What are you *doing*?" Am I yelling? I'm louder than I should be. But for the love of all things great and good in this world, he can't become a mess.

Tom's face hardens. "I took a nap."

"Of *course* you took a nap. What else are you going to do? Maybe work? Maybe take those pictures of the wall?" I point at the arch between the studio space and the dining room. "Maybe shower?"

He doesn't say anything. He doesn't respond at all. He just stands there and stares at the back of his easel.

"Tom?" I take a step toward him. The men in his family have taken enough crap in their lifetimes to break anyone's back, but they all got up and moved forward. This shouldn't be so tough for him. He just lost a job he didn't want in the first place. No one died the way his mother and sister did. No one ended up in a burn ward for months like Dan. No one got knifed in the gut the way Rob did this past spring.

Tom taps the side of his head, then points at the easel. "Nothing's coming to me."

"So you took a nap?" I am still yelling? Why am I yelling?

I'm shaking, too. This can't be happening. He can't descend this way. He's the lucky Quidell. The one shit bypasses. The one who's there for his brothers when they need him because he's the one with room left on his shoulders to take the burden.

The way he helped me, when we met. He's my mooring in the storm. He's everyone's mooring. But now he's drifting.

I think I finally understand what's terrifying me about all this. He's lost his footing, and he's accidently swept mine out from under me.

"Juri wants a meeting." Maybe giving him focus will help. "His text says they have gallery space in their Vegas hotel. Actual gallery space, Tom." I hold out my phone. "It's not selling out."

He sighs and rubs his belly. Then he shakes his head and walks toward the kitchen. "I don't like you talking to him," he mumbles.

"Excuse me?" What the hell did *that* mean?

Tom glances over his shoulder. "He's a predator, Sammie."

"Since when have you thought of me as prey?" I flick on the light as I follow him into the dark kitchen. "And how do you know Juri's a predator? You've never met him!"

He squints and rubs his eyes when the overhead light winks on. "They're all predators."

I'm at a loss for words. "Are you being possessive, Thomas Quidell?" I don't know what else to ask.

Tom chuckles. "Of course I am." But his face says his response is more out of expectation than because he actually believes it.

"I can take care of myself." I can.

Tom picks up a dish and tosses it willy-nilly into the top rack of the dishwasher. He's moving like a little boy convinced that if he's shitty at his chores, he'll get out of having to do them again because everyone will get sick of having to clean up after him.

"You're acting like Bart." Though his nephew has better manners.

Tom leans against the sink. "All I did was take a goddamned nap. Why is that a problem?"

"The nap's not the problem. The 'I don't give a shit' attitude is."

His eyes narrow again and that hard face reappears. "Nothing's *coming*." He taps his chest. "I have writer's block." He looks up at the ceiling. "Painter's block."

"How often do you get painter's block?" Because this is the first time in the year we've been together that he's said one word about blocking. That he hasn't just picked up a sketch book and drawn what's in front of him even if he feels down. Or asked me to take off my clothes and pose so that he can work through a composition issue.

"Do you want to draw tonight?" I point out at the studio. "I'll set up the blankets." We've talked about getting a settee or one of those old-time fainting couches for me, but I haven't had time to check out antique stores.

He stares over my shoulder for a long moment. "He's a predator, Sammie. I don't think you should meet with him." Then he shakes as if whatever dream's been haunting him since he walked out of the bedroom suddenly releases from his skin.

"Why?" But I don't think Tom fully understands.

He silently drops another cup into the dishwasher.

"Tom, why?" I touch his arm, then his back. He's carrying more tension than he usually does, and I suspect he hurts.

But that doesn't mean he can act jealous.

"Because I don't want to be part of his corporate world, okay?" He waves me off. "I don't want to do that again."

"This is different." It is. "The only corporate part is who owns the gallery."

He looks up at the ceiling again. "Seriously? Your ex-boyfriend is a super-rich douchebag and you think the only relevant bit of information here is that he *promises* to be hands-off?"

I don't know if Juri will be hands-off or not. "We haven't talked specifics. I can be firm with him. Make sure he understands that he's dealing with a real artist and not one of his lackeys." I touch Tom's arm again. "Just let me deal with him. He'll take your scowling as a challenge."

"*Predator*." Tom clenches his teeth.

I step back. "Don't be melodramatic."

Tom picks up a plate as if he's going to whip it at the wall, but he stops. His fingers tighten around its lip for a second, then he carefully sets it down. "Please don't meet with him." He rubs his forehead.

"He knows a lot of people, Tom. His contacts are as good as Andy's. Better, actually. Even if the Las Vegas hotel doesn't work out, I can get intel on other options."

Tom closes his eyes. "There's nothing I can say, is there?"

"I don't understand what the problem is." I don't. Juri is not the threat Tom thinks he is, though the real threat here might not be Juri so much as his corporation.

Which is frankly stupid. So my mind circles back to the obvious: jealousy.

"I'm not going to fuck him, Tom." I throw my hands into the air. "He's not going to force me to do anything I don't want to do. He's not a bad guy."

Tom looks like he doesn't believe me. "I don't want this."

Then he's gone, through the door, and stomping down the hall toward the bedroom.

"Tom!" I yell.

He rips his t-shirt over his head and drops it on the bed. "I need some air."

"So that's it, huh? You're going full-metal stubborn Quidell on me?" I pick up his t-shirt and throw it at his head. "Didn't you learn anything from watching Dan use his pain as a firewall? You need to trust—"

His phone rings.

CHAPTER 12

Thomas

I swipe my phone off the dresser without answering Sammie. "It's Rob." I hold up my hand.

Am I latching onto my little brother's distraction? I can't shake the odd, vibrating feeling left over from my nap. And the strange certainty that something is *wrong*.

My teeth grind against each other. I realize I'm clenching my jaw.

The phone rings again.

"Call him back later!" Sammie looks like she wants to throw the pillows at my head.

I swipe to answer.

"Isa needs to talk to Sammie," I say more to my fiancé than to my brother. Maybe they can talk some sense into each other.

I don't want Sammie dealing with a man my gut tells me is a predator. Maybe not on a personal level—maybe my jealousy *is* causing a portion of my reaction—but more on a metaphysical, soul-eating level.

In an off-sync, vibrating, dreamlike kind of way. Ghostly. Ethereal. I can handle work-for-hire. Illustration is all work-for-hire. I just don't want to feed a vampire if it means waking up from nightmares every day.

"She found a lead and—"

"Tom," my brother says. I hear shuffling and the sound of a bag zipping. "Dad had a heart attack. We're leaving now."

"What?" The child inside of me, the kid who used to spend all his free time in his dad's studio drawing and painting and imitating, screams *That's not fair!*

Not Dad, too.

"When?" I turn on my phone's speaker so Sammie can hear. "Dad had a heart attack," I say to her.

She touches her fingers to her lips. "How bad is it?"

All thoughts of Juri Olson drop away. Am I about to lose another parent to a stupid, sneaky, bullshit reason?

"About two hours ago. His friend Sal called." More shuffling and zipping crackles through my phone's speaker. "They put in a stent. He's in intensive care but he's responsive."

My breath rushes out of my lungs as one big exhale. At least he's able to communicate. "What did the docs say?"

"I don't know yet." My little brother sounds frantic. "Isa's talking to Camille. Dan can't fly down until Thursday. Not with her home sick. He also has a major state inspection he can't miss on Thursday morning. He'll come directly after."

"I might not be able to take you to the airport tomorrow." Sammie swipes at her own phone. "I could ask Andy."

"We're leaving now. We'll drive what we can tonight and be in Sedona as soon as possible," Rob says.

"Camille wants to talk to you about flights," Isa yells.

The next half hour is one call after another. Plans manifest and plans fizzle away. But by the end, I'm booked on an early flight to Phoenix tomorrow morning. Dan will take me to the airport, but it would help if he didn't have to pick me up in the morning, so Sammie agreed to drop me at his house tonight.

The drive to my brother's takes the same half hour it always takes. Streets to freeway to streets again, and here we are, sitting in the cab of my truck at the end of Dan's driveway, my window rolled down and my body not doing anything.

And all I can think is *I'm confused.*

I feel as if I'm inside one of the huge particle accelerators they talk about in science news. The kilometer-wide, circular tunnels physicists use to spin up wee bits of matter until they're moving at the speed of light.

Then they crash those bits together.

My gut's a particle accelerator and now the free-for-all is spraying all over my life. Bits of me are hitting all my muscles like shrapnel. I'm breaking myself down simply by working myself up.

Sammie pulls the key from the ignition. "I'll pick you up Sunday." She squeezes my thigh. "If you need to stay longer, then stay longer, okay? I'll field any editor inquiries that might come in."

She doesn't say anything about meeting with Juri Olson.

No need to worry me. I smile and squeeze her fingers. She has it under control.

Which she does, yet I'm going to worry anyway. I can't help it. It'll keep me from worrying about my dad.

The entire drive, I tried to figure out what's wrong with me. Why I'm angry. Why I want to run away and not look back, or forward, or sideways. Why I don't care if I finish my forest-and-gully dreams painting.

Why I feel so numb about Dad being in the hospital.

Maybe I should just take up Dan's offer of a job. At least I'd be up and moving around. My body would care about something.

I haven't worked out in over a week. Haven't eaten anything but cereal and peanut butter. It's like I'm a kid and Dad's gone off on a trip and left me to fend for myself. I won't burn down the house but God knows I'm not going to make my bed.

Except Dad's in the hospital and I need to act like the adult I am.

I lay my head against my seat's headrest. Down the street, a couple of older kids play in a yard. They yell and scream, and a big bright yellow ball rolls out into the street. The largest kid stops at the curb, looks both ways, then dashes out to retrieve the toy.

It's always the oldest and most mature who takes care of the younger ones, isn't it? Dan's always taken care of Rob and me. Always made sure we were fed and clothed. He used to take us school supply shopping even after he married his ex. But now he needs us to help take care of Dad.

The last of the summer heat and humidity isn't all that bad. The evening drapes itself over my brother's suburban neighborhood. This place is sweet. It's safe. It's where a family should be. These kids, I'm sure, do make their beds each morning.

I used to live here. I helped with Bart while Dan worked the long hours. At the time, I thought it necessary but constraining. Now I'm just glad I'm not paying his mortgage, as well.

Except Dan paid off the house with the settlement money after his accident. He remodeled too, and Bart now has an excellent suburban life with his excellent, suburban parents.

I open the door. Time to stand up and go through the motions.

The front curtains flutter. Camille's face appears, then her hand, waving me in.

Like Sammie, Camille is a beautiful woman, though unlike Sammie, I've never gotten the sense that Camille cared about the primping and the makeup. She's down-to-Earth in that I'm more likely to find her in sweats and swimming inside one of Dan's old t-shirts than I am to ever see her in a skirt and heels.

"She says her fever broke this morning, but don't get too close, okay?" Sammie frowns in the house's general direction.

I doubt Dan will be flying down on Thursday. I suspect he'll be nursing his own fever, as will Bart.

My nephew appears in the front window, a big smile on his almost six-year-old face. I wave. He bounces. I suspect he'll soon be out on the driveway, even if he knows he should behave.

I lean across the truck's console and kiss Sammie. "I'll text you when I get to the airport."

She nods and touches my cheek. "Be safe."

I kiss her again.

"Don't lick Camille, either, okay?"

I chuckle. "You are the only woman I lick."

She chuckles, too. "Take care of your Dad." One last kiss lands on my cheek. "Take care of yourself."

I unfold myself from the passenger seat and grab my bag from behind the seat. One last wave, and I make my way up the driveway to my brother's front door.

I stretch my neck to loosen my muscles and maybe release some of the ache, and do my best to smile. Can't be crabby when I'm around Bart. It wouldn't do him—or me—any good.

He launches himself at me the moment I walk through the door. "Uncle Tommy!"

"Whoa, there, big guy." I scoop him up.

Camille, in a big, fluffy, bright pink robe, sits on the steps up to the second floor. She looks ghostly and dehydrated, and probably shouldn't be here alone with Bart, but Dan had a late meeting. She grins and wipes her nose with a tissue. "He knows he's to stay at least ten feet from me at all times unless I specifically ask him for help."

Bart hugs my neck, then squirms because, I think, he's remembered that he's a big kid now who thinks no one should carry him around. I set him down and he immediately stands tall. "Mommy says I'm to use my hand sanitizer *all the time*." He scoops two bottles off the table. "This one is for you!" He hands one to me.

I glance at Camille. She shrugs. "The bed downstairs needs sheets." She leans against the wall.

"I'll take care of it." I'm beginning to wonder if Dan asked me to come over more to watch Camille than because he didn't have time to pick me up tomorrow morning. "How are you feeling?"

She shrugs again. "I'll be fine by Thursday." Another sniffle and another nose wipe follow. "I'm over the worst of it. Dan and Bart aren't showing symptoms, so there's hope."

"Go upstairs." I point at my nephew. "Bart will fill me in on what needs doing yet tonight."

Bart salutes. "I've been taking care of Mommy." He flicks open his hand sanitizer and slathers on a thick layer.

Camille grins and shakes her head. Slowly, she hauls herself to her feet. "Yell if you need anything." She glances over her shoulder. "Dan will be home soon."

I wave her away. She turns to ascend the stairs, a sniffling woman inside a pink puffball.

Bart immediately scoops a couple of action figures off the coffee table. "Do you want to play heroes with me?" He holds out a new character I don't recognize from one of the big summer blockbusters.

Bart looks up at me with his blue eyes. He doesn't have to deal with life. He can use his imagination and go someplace better.

I drop onto the couch. "Sure."

Camille's head appears around the corner of the stairs. Bart looks at her, then at me, then back at her. Then he runs for the steps, but stops outside of sneeze range. "I love you, Mommy," he says. He's back to me and the action figures before she blinks.

Her look softens, but a certain complexity creeps over her face as if she's running scenarios she doesn't want to voice in front of Bart.

A finger swirls in my nephew's general direction. "You, young man, need to get ready for bed. You have school tomorrow."

"Yes, Mommy." Bart buzzes his lips and dances an action figure dressed all in black across the table. "No one beats the dragons!" he declares, and bounces the figure down the table toward a brightly painted mythical beast.

I look up at Camille. Some of her normal happiness reappears in her eyes as she watches Bart, but it vanishes quickly when she sniffles again.

"He needs to brush his teeth." She glances up the steps. "He can stay up until his daddy gets home but he needs to be ready for bed."

Bart leans his action figure and the dragon against each other. "But we don't want to go to bed."

Camille rolls her eyes. "Bed, young man. Okay?"

"Yes, Mommy." Bart dances his toys across the table again.

Camille nods toward me and finally disappears up the stairs.

And I wonder if maybe I should have made Dan pick me up in the morning instead of coming over here tonight. But that would have made *his* life more difficult, and at this point, I need to help, not hinder.

Bart looks up at me, crosses his arms over his chest, and makes an exaggerated *humphing* frown. I look down at my own arms. I'm in the exact same posture.

I'm not sure if the sound coming from my throat is a laugh or a cry, but Bart seems to think it's funny. He points a finger and laughs his little kid ass off.

Then he scoops his action figure and his dragon off the table and runs for the stairs. "Come on, Uncle Tommy!"

I guess it's time for the little things in life. Time to brush our teeth.

CHAPTER 13

Thomas

Dan hands me a beer, then pops the top off his own. We stand in his kitchen, him leaning against the counter next to the fridge and me against the counter next to the stove.

When problems get sorted at Dan's house, it's usually in the kitchen.

He's not only older—he's larger, too. Dan is one of the few people other than our father who is noticeably taller and broader than me. We both have the same ocean blue-green eyes, though his hair is darker than mine. Not as dark as Rob's, but he inherited a depth of color from Mom that I did not.

Not long ago, he and Camille had an issue-filled moment. Dan is "dealing with it." He goes to a multitude of therapists on a regular basis now—physical for his shoulder and leg, psych for all the shit his ex ladled onto him, and a massage therapist who keeps the muscles working—all with the blessing and encouragement of his girlfriend.

He doesn't say anything, just stares at his kitchen floor and leans against his fridge as he takes a pull at his beer.

"We knew we'd have to deal with this sooner or later," he says. "Dad's at that age."

Rickety joints, heart attacks, slow and wasting horrors. They come for everyone, even our father. Dan looks down at the floor again, but his fingers rub the label on the bottle. "I was thinking of taking Bart and Camille down for Thanksgiving."

None of us handled the aftermath of Mom's and Jeanie's deaths well. We still don't, even after a decade. That's why Dad's not here. He moved away right after Dan's release from the burn ward. Rob had started college and moved out, and I had moved in with Dan to help with Bart. Dad sold the house we grew up in and vanished into the dry heat of Sedona, Arizona.

He showed up for a couple of weeks while Rob convalesced, but then he was gone again. I always figured he couldn't look at his sons without thinking about his wife and his daughter.

I have a hard time looking at *him* and not thinking about my mother and my sister.

That odd, pained feeling lands in my gut again.

Dan picks at his beer bottle label. "I wish he would have stayed here." He closes his eyes and rubs his forehead. "We could have looked after him."

Probably not, I think. When Dad left, Dan was barely holding it together, between his injury and raising Bart by himself. Rob was a freshman. I was a sophomore. None of us were in any position to care for a father with major depression.

But Dan's the family man. Dan would have figured out how to deal with the problem even if our father didn't want it dealt with.

"I'll stay in Sedona as long as one of us needs to be there." I'm the unemployed son. The one with the "free time." So I guess it gets to be me.

Dan sighs. It's a full-on, deep, all-his-breath kind of sigh. The kind he only does when he feels vulnerable—which doesn't happen often. When it does, it's usually held in.

Maybe the therapy is doing its job.

Dan looks me in the eye. Vulnerability dances through the muscles around his eyes and his mouth. He held Rob and me together after

Mom died. He survived a crazy bitch ex-wife. He spent three months in the hospital and now he's rebuilding his life with his son and a woman who loves him.

And now we might lose our other parent.

"Camille is still sick." He rubs his forehead again. "The fever's gone but she's not going to be one hundred percent for a few days." He looks up at me again. "I hope Bart doesn't catch it."

"Or you."

Dan chuckles. "I probably should stay out of Dad's hospital room until I'm past the incubation period, huh?"

I clasp his shoulder. "Probably."

He nods and takes another sip of his beer. "How's the job hunt going?"

The muscles of my own face pull and tighten in what I know is a mirror image of what I just saw play across my brother's. My breath pushes up. I sigh in very much the same way, and slump against the counter.

There's a rawness to Dan and me. Rob too, but it's different with him. He's brilliant and a smartass and better at turning whatever is abrading his soul outward toward the universe. Dan sucks it in and spins it tight. Me, I paint.

"I should be producing." I absently tap my bottle against the counter.

"Well, yeah." Dan takes another sip.

"Sammie's pushing me." It's not her fault I'm blocked, nor is it her fault that I don't want her dealing with a predator.

My unease is my own.

"To do what?" Dan stands up straight and plugs his phone into its charger.

"The obvious." I stand straight as well. "Work on networking. Paint something salable. Get dressed in the morning and put my cereal bowls in the dishwasher when I'm done eating."

Dan chuckles. "When we were up at the lake, Rob commented on how he thought you and Sammie looked a little... haggard."

My fingers go back to tapping my bottle on the countertop. I glance down at my hand and will them to stop. "We've both been working long hours since Andy helped her set up my gallery show."

"Gotta keep with the producing, right?" Dan salutes with his beer.

"Dad used to say the same thing." Pretty much every day. He'd paint and draw for two hours, then spend an hour taking care of us, then work for another two, then take another hour, then work three more, then put us to bed.

Both he and Mom worked into the evening on the business of being an artist. I never realized how intense the business side was until Sammie set up the first show. I knew, intellectually. I'd seen it first-hand, but I didn't understand.

Now she wants to make a deal with a rich devil. We might come out of the deal comfortable. We might not.

I might lose a chunk of my soul in the process.

And I cannot shake the feeling that I'm about to get crushed under primordial plants and concrete concourses.

"Sammie's got a meeting set up with the Olson Companies." I stare at my beer bottle.

Dan opens and closes his mouth. "For what?"

"Seems they just bought a chain of resorts." Not the same chain Dan is working with. A bigger, glitzier chain of international hotels. "It's a huge deal. Destinations and shit like that."

For a second, I think Dan might be jealous.

"She used to date Juri Olson," I say. And I can't help but wonder what part of *her* soul she might lose with this deal.

The shock of the name drop pulls Dan out of his daze. "*The* Juri Olson? The son of the founder? *That* guy?"

I nod *yes*. "They're putting in a gallery in their Vegas hotel and he wants youth-oriented media and art." I roll my eyes.

"You said yes to this, right?" I can see the gears going behind his eyes. "A deal with them could set you up for life."

I swirl my beer. "She used to *date* him, Dan."

"So?" Dan takes a sip of his beer. "Don't be an idiot."

His face clearly shows what he's thinking: I'm childish because he thinks I'm comparing myself to Sammie's Prince Charming. That I have a deep-seated fear Mr. Juri Olson will decide he wants Sammie back and that there won't be a damned thing anyone will be able to do about it.

Not her. Not me. Not the world. No one.

Maybe Dan's right. Maybe I'm being an idiot. Or maybe I'm living the old story of the goddess who chooses love instead of wealth. I won't lose Sammie. But that doesn't mean I won't spend my life wondering if my *not* losing her is temporary because she's hungry.

Thing is, no one talks about the aftermath of a choice like that. The chronic, lifelong knowledge that she sacrificed to be with me, and that her sacrifice wasn't small.

Perhaps I'm pissed because she won't do what I want her to do, which is not go to the meeting. Or perhaps I'm mad at myself for being immature enough to ask in the first place.

I take a long pull on my beer.

"So I take it you haven't found a job yet." Dan's voice betrays a level of impatience I rarely hear from him anymore.

"No." I take another sip. "Editors work in epochs, not weeks."

Dan chuckles. "Completed any new pieces?" He waves his hand. "To refresh your gallery space?"

That's not how it works with the gallery, but I don't need to go into that. Besides, Sammie handles that end of the business.

I look up at the ceiling. "I am so confused."

Dan chuckles again. "No shit, little brother." He pats my shoulder. "Welcome to adulthood."

"I don't think I like adulting, big brother."

Now Dan laughs. "Get some rest."

I nod, thankful that Dan doesn't feel the need to berate me.

Sleeping in my old bed in his basement, at least for one night, feels like a clean slate, but is it because I'm away from my studio or because I'm away from Sammie's can-do work ethic?

"I'll pay you back for the plane ticket," I say. It seems to be the correct way to adult. "Once the paying work starts up again."

Dan tosses his bottle into the recycling. "I have frequent flyer miles. It's not a problem."

No matter how old we get, or how similar in height and size, or how father-oriented he might be, he will always be my big brother.

"Rob says Dad's responsive. He's going to be fine." My brother seems to say his words more for himself than for me, but he grins when he looks me in the eye. "Maybe Dad will have leads he's willing to share." Dan tosses my empty bottle into the recycling too. "Look at it this way: You make progress in your relationship with Dad, maybe it'll help you make progress in other areas, as well."

I shake my head. "Did your therapist tell you that?" Sounds like a bunch of New Age mumblings to me—and something Dad might buy into. He's always had a mystical streak. More "portents" and "signs" and "feelings" than anything dogma-oriented. It was never a problem, and our mother tolerated it. Sometimes she even found Dad's "seeing" of auras and "feeling" of ghosts as sweet.

Dan, Rob, and I ignored it.

Dan shrugs. "Massage therapist. She says to remember about snowballs and hills." He whistles as he pantomimes a ball picking up speed as it rolls down a slope. "A little encouragement and a bit of success never hurt anyone."

He grins and nods toward the living room. "I have an early meeting tomorrow." He yawns and rubs at his shoulder. "If the contract I have now pans out and I go national with the hotel chain I'm subcontracting with, I *will* need help." He gives me a quick glance.

I shake my head. "I'd be more of a hindrance than a help, dear brother."

Dan frowns. "I've been talking to Jason about coming on full-time, but he would lose his disability support." He glances out the window. "He's also concerned about interacting with customers."

Jason was the other firefighter who was hurt at the same time as Dan. Jason ended up with nerve damage and a traumatic brain injury. He's now one of the "hidden" disabled—he looks fit and healthy, but he has issues talking.

Dan's been helping out where he can, but my brother is only one man.

"I'm sure you and Jason can figure out how to make it work." I shrug, too. "Sammie might be able to help. Hell, Andy's good at figuring out how to make an environment work for people." He's a freakin' genius at it.

"It'd be a major success for Jason if he could work with me." Dan checks his phone to make sure it's charging before ushering me out of the kitchen. "But a major success needs a lot of little successes in front to fuel its snowballing."

My brain immediately makes an animation of a giant snowball crushing little children "successes" as it rolls down a hill. They all flail their little successful arms and shriek like little banshees as the big snowball eats them whole.

I stop in the arch between his kitchen and the dining area. "I'm not sure that metaphor's working."

Dan laughs. "Shakespeare, I am not."

Dan pats me on the back one last time and I descend into his basement for my last restless night of sleep before flying into my father's realm.

CHAPTER 14

Samantha

A text from Tom appears on my phone: *Good night*.
I lean against the wide window in Tom's studio and brush at my swollen eyes. I'm going to walk into work tomorrow looking like shit.

Tom left one of his drop cloths in a wadded up heap under his easel and his pencils out in piles on his drafting table. A dirty cereal bowl sits precariously on the table's edge just waiting for Mickles to knock it onto the floor.

I turned off most of the lights. I don't know why.

Tom's father might be dying but all I want is to batter Tom's shoulder with my fists and bite his earlobes because we didn't really settle the fight. Not really. So now it's going to simmer.

I want him to say sorry and give me the best make-up sex of both our lives. But I know that's selfish. *He's* selfish. I'm selfish.

And confused.

I've never met his father. His brothers are more important to him, as is Bart. I don't pry. I figure, like his art, he'll explain someday.

But maybe I should pry. Maybe I should ask him to clearly articulate what's making him angry. Dad, job, painter's block, me... I don't know. And now I won't be able to ask until he returns from Arizona.

Does he honestly think I'd go back to Juri Olson? We didn't have a real relationship. It wasn't anything close to real. I never had a real relationship until I met Tom.

I wish Tom understood how precious he is to me.

A tear lands on my phone.

The giant painting glows in the last of the evening light, the one with the dreamy plants and the odd, crushing hordes in a concrete valley. I don't understand what it means, but I do get a sense of what it represents.

And why he stopped working on it when he lost his job.

Why the hell didn't I see it before? It's been here, all along, right in front of me. He needs success.

I look down at my phone.

Good night, I tap in.

I'll text tomorrow once I'm through security.

Camille already forwarded Tom's flight info. I stare at my phone's screen for a long moment. Reflections flow across the studio space, light thrown by cars passing by below, on the street, and for a brief second, I can't see anything at all.

Not the information on my phone. Not Tom's painting. Not my own intent.

My stomach growls. Mickles meows. I should feed us both but I don't feel like rummaging for leftover pizza or a bowl of cereal.

Cereal.

What do I say to Tom? Do what you need to do? Please come home?

I love you. I don't know what else to text him. Or to say. What else can I say? Nothing seems to be getting through his wall of... what? Doubt? Anger? Masculine stubbornness?

I love you, too, appears. *Get some sleep*.

I set my phone next to Tom's dirty cereal dish. A car passes by on the street below the window. Someone yells, and someone else laughs.

They move on by, but my eye is drawn back to the concrete-looking, hallway-ish gullies snaking through Tom's huge painting. He's outlined people in there, but they're not people, and I don't think they're meant to be fully human.

The few strokes he's laid down flow in an Impressionistic manner, but more precise. It's as if there's a sense that he needs to be robotic. Not that he is, or that he wants to be, but that precision is necessary to give the painting the correct level of blurriness.

A bus grumbles by and I look at the window. The lights from the business across the street blink green and blue. Bright reds dot the reflections cast onto our expensive floor.

And I wonder if this world is what Tom truly wants. I also wonder if he knows what he wants.

I look back at the painting. I wish he'd finish it. My gut's telling me that he's got something here.

How can I help? *Should* I help? We have, after all, a real relationship. Aren't we supposed to rely on each other? He needs a solid foundation. How else will he be able to create?

What if he doesn't trust me to build with him what he needs?

What about what I need?

Slowly, I inhale all the way to the base of my lungs, and just as slowly, I exhale. And as the air leaves my lungs, I wonder about the empty place left behind. Do I trust myself to build that foundation?

Mickles saunters into the studio. He does his leaning walk—the "I'm going to rub on your leg" tip and arched back all cats do a good three feet out before actually making contact—and throws his fluffy side against my calf.

He sits on my foot and looks at my face.

I pick him up. He head-butts my chin and erupts in a generous purr.

The cat knows what he wants. The cat adapts to the environment he's in. Noisy, silent, full of vermin, pristine—Mr. Pickles handles it all. And Mr. Pickles does it with confidence.

"I can handle Juri Olson," I say.

Mickles responds with a sweet meow.

I glance at my phone again. Tom isn't the only artist I rep. "What do you think, kitty? Should we call Isa?" Maybe Tom's sister-in-law can lead by example.

Mickles meows again. I set him on the floor and swipe my phone off Tom's drafting table.

I'll eat later. Time to work.

CHAPTER 15

Thomas

Sky Harbor International Airport in Phoenix is a massive sprawling complex of interconnected shopping malls interspersed with the occasional boarding gate. At least the people are friendly and it's well lit, except for the baggage pick-up area. How can an airport in the brightest, hottest part of the nation have an entire subsection that feels like a dank cave?

I check out the native art in a showcase between carousels six and seven while I wait for my bag. The hypnotic, colorful beadwork twirls up in my gut in much the same way as one of the paintings back home in the Art Institute does. There's one in particular, a Kandinsky with the strong lines and the blue tones. The beadwork pulls up the same way, twisting along its geometry, and the same ghostly sense of history oozes from its edges.

I want to run my fingers over the patterns and the wrinkled leather. To breathe in the dust gathered in its weave. To be part of its ritual and moment in time.

Seeing this piece behind glass gives me the same subtle sense of disgust I feel when I see an exquisite butterfly pinned inside a case.

My phone trills and a message from my dad's friend, Sal, appears. *Outside door thirteen*, it says. *Green Accord.*

I'm about to be picked up by a lady who goes by the name "Sal" and who looks like she could kick six-two me to the other side of the state of Arizona.

Thing is, from her photo, I don't think I'm about to meet a physically large woman, or one who stands out in a crowd, but she definitely has the aura of someone you shouldn't mess with.

Behind me, the bell sounds as my carousel starts. *Out in a minute*, I text back. *Getting my bag.*

All right.

I half expect a *young man* added on for good measure, but it seems Sal is a woman of manners.

I pull my bag and walk the length of Sky Harbor's cavernous lower level toward door thirteen. Home had been a comfortable-if-warm summer day, not too hot or humid. Phoenix in the summer is anything but comfortable. I hold my breath as I walk through the sliding doors into the desert heat.

I swear I hear the difference in the air as it slaps me full across the face. Arizona sounds like the blast furnace it is. It's hard to breathe. It's hard to keep my eyes open because I feel as if they're going to burst in my skull.

Sedona should be a good fifteen degrees cooler, so at least we'll be driving away from the "fry an egg on my forehead" temperatures.

I spot the green Accord and wave. A woman unfolds from the driver's side—no one in their right mind would wait on the concrete walk in air that is ten degrees hotter than their body temperature—and carefully tries not to touch her car's metal exterior. She's about Sammie's size, maybe slightly smaller, with an interesting hourglass-inside-a-rectangle shape.

Sal's shoulders and hips line up perfectly. Her high waist curves in just exactly where it should for a beautiful form. Her breasts are just large enough that if I were to draw an outline version of her, their sweep would break up the lines of her arms nicely.

My dad's buddy is the perfect figure model.

When her gaze lands on me, I still feel as if she could kick my ass

87

to California if she wanted to. Must be the piercing expression. Or maybe it's how she takes in the cars and people around us. For a second, I wonder if she's some type of law enforcement.

Sal looks me up and down and I swear she just read my entire life from how I'm carrying my bag, and, once again, I wonder what she does for a living. The gray in her short hair stands out against the black and adds a hint of cop, but she moves more like a dancer than a fighter.

Sal's nose twitches and she tips her head ever so slightly, then smiles and holds out her arms. "You must be Thomas!"

The hug is quick with the correct amount of air between us. "You're Sal?" I ask.

"Sal Martin." She pats my shoulder and pops the trunk on the Accord. "You look just like your father."

She looks to be about ten, maybe fifteen years younger than my dad, but to be honest, I can't tell. She's less weathered than I expected, and could be ten years older, for all I know. But she was kind enough to make the five-hour round trip to fetch her friend's wayward son from the Phoenix airport, so I shouldn't complain.

I drop my bag into the trunk of her Accord. "My older brother looks more like Dad than I do."

Sal chuckles. "You walk like him." She waves toward the passenger side. "In you go before we both melt."

I dutifully duck my head under the frame and cram myself into the sedan.

"Nothing had changed with Jeremiah when I left." Sal watches and I can't tell if she's amused or if she feels my now-cramped pain.

"I talked to Isa." Sal waves at the car's roof. "Last I heard, your brother and his wife had stopped in Vegas for lunch."

The seat is all the way back already, thank all that's good in the world. "Isa's morning sickness has slowed them down." They should arrive around the same time as Sal and me.

I twist in my cramped legs and pull closed the door. "I drive a truck."

Sal shakes her head and starts up the car.

With traffic, it takes a good hour to clear Phoenix. Sal makes small talk about Dad's local gallery show, and her campground and resort.

"Resort only in that the restaurant down the street runs a deal for my guests on Thursday nights."

She doesn't show a lot of worry and I can't tell if it's because she's a good actor of if she is genuinely not upset about the circumstances that brought me to Arizona.

"Tests still needed running," she says, "but the stent is in and your dad's groggy."

I ask about the local color. We talk about the art scene and the New Age glitz that I suspect drew Dad to Sedona in the first place. By the time we pull into Dad's driveway, I think Sal and I might turn out to be pretty good traveling companions.

The sun hangs low and the reddish-orange glow of the mountains spreads over the city and gives Dad's little house a salmon tint. It looks exactly the same as it did the last time I visited, which was before Dan's injury.

I pull my bag out of the Accord's trunk. Sal jumps a little where she stands at the front fender—mostly, I suspect, to shake out the stiffness of the long drive.

The plane plus the cramped car have left a knot in my lower back. I should probably go for a run once the sun's down.

"Come." She waves me toward the door as she pulls a key from her pocket. "Let's get you settled. Then I'll take you over to the hospital."

I shade my eyes as we walk the concrete ribbon to the front door. The hills here add a glint of deep red burgundy to her Accord's shimmering green.

It's dusty here. All deserts are dusty; the grit and fine abrasive film were what I noticed first about Las Vegas the one and only time I visited while an undergrad. Dust, glare, heat, and a massive draw on the power grid, all with a nice crust of tourist insincerity.

Do I really want to show my work in a tourist factory? Does it really matter?

I really am confused.

I drop my bag on a chair next to the door. Dad's place is small and dark on the inside. Sammie would hate that he keeps the curtains drawn; he always said it helps to keep the interior cool in the summer. A television sits in the corner along with an overstuffed sofa and a chair, and the dining room table we had as kids takes up the entire area in front of his tiny, open kitchen.

The curtains over his large patio door stand open, though, and low light filters in over the same yellowing tablecloth my mom always used to cover the table.

There's a reason for the tablecloth. I used to paint there, as a child. Some stains never come out.

On the table, a closed laptop covered with papers sits next to a dirty plate, a pile of sketch pads, and an older camera.

Sal scoops up the plate as she walks toward the kitchen. "Do you want something to eat?" She taps the front of the fridge. "You should eat before going over. The canteen at the hospital is woefully unacceptable."

I walk toward her and the kitchen. My stomach growls; airline peanuts aren't nearly enough to eat on a three-and-a-half-hour plane trip. "Do you mind if I eat in your car?"

Sal sets the plate in the sink. "Drop your stuff in the guest room and get cleaned up. I'll make you a sandwich you can bring with you."

Sal digs around in the fridge. "For such a large man, your father sure doesn't have a lot of food in the house." She taps her finger on the door handle again. "We should pick up groceries."

Sal sets peanut butter next to a box of snickerdoodles on the counter, then begins what might be a futile search for bread. "Get cleaned up." Sal looks up at me. "He'll be fine, Tom."

But I don't think she believes it any more than I do.

CHAPTER 16

Thomas

Sedona's hospital is a low-slung, desert-colored, concrete slab. Dry trees and bushes with gray-green leaves and brittle branches surround the entrance. Tall black signs proclaiming this "Care" and that "Care" point up one walk or another.

Sal parks her Accord in the lot beyond the covered drive in front of the Emergency entrance, and when she turns off the engine, the evening's remaining heat crawls in through vents and the cracks around the doors.

The hospital is remarkably quiet. Only a handful of other cars wait in the parking lot. The building's entrances glow like white fires in the naturally golden landscape. The air smells less dusty here, but more medicinal, even outside.

We walk toward the main entrance, which shares doors with Emergency, and I wonder if this small, rural hospital is the best place for an older man with a stent in his heart.

Sal pulls out her wallet. "The guard will want to see ID," she says as the door swishes open.

I dutifully pull out my license for the bored middle-aged guy sitting behind the desk. His hands are as round as his head and belly, and his gray-blue security guard polo shirt looks uncomfortable and itchy.

We sign in. The guard checks our IDs against what I assume is a no-admittance database, snaps a picture, and prints off a "Hello, my name is..." badge for each of us.

"You two know where to go?" He points down the hallway behind him before either of us can answer. "Check in at the nurses' station."

We pad down the hallway. Sal squeezes my elbow before nodding toward the nurses. "I'll wait out here," she says, and ushers me into Dad's room.

Machines beep. Indicators flash. The overhead lights are on low and I blink to allow my eyes to compensate.

The room smells more of conditioned air and the dust outside than it does of medicine and microbe-killing swabs. An adobe-red vinyl chair sits in the corner next to the bed, and an adjustable table next to the window.

A nurse is checking Dad's IV and his vitals when I come in, even though the bed is some new medical robo-wonder that measures all sorts of data.

She's an angular woman, thin with high cheekbones and a Native American face. She wears her black hair as a long, tight, well-managed braid and her blue-gray scrubs as loose, slightly-askew, rolled-up armor.

The whiteboard on the wall next to the door says her name is Alma. Watching her move around the bed makes me glad that even though Sedona is rural Arizona, it still attracts health workers who seem to care about their jobs.

"You're one of Mr. Quidell's sons?" she asks.

Dad sighs in his sleep while she carefully checks his pulse.

"Tom," I say. "My brother Rob will be here later tonight and Dan will fly down at the end of the week." Though at this point, I don't think Rob and Isa will make visiting hours.

Alma throws me a quick grin. "You look like him."

I grin back at her. "I do." I don't feel up to the rest of this conversation—"but not as much as Dan"—which is usually followed with a long comparison of my life with my more stable brother's.

"Are you the artist?" She nods toward the door as she moved

around Dad's bed. "Ms. Martin said Mr. Quidell's artist son would be here today."

"Yes," I say. I don't want to have this conversation, either. I don't want to explain my lack-of-work to someone I just met.

Alma seems to understand. She stands at the foot of Dad's bed with her hands in her pockets. "Do you need anything?" She nods toward the door. "Don't have much time before visiting hours are over."

No, I don't. About forty-five minutes. "I'm good."

"It's important that he sleep," she says. "The sedative will wear off and he'll be awake and ready for visitors tomorrow morning." She grins again. "Are you sure you don't need anything? A glass of water?"

I shake my head *no*. Alma checks Dad one more time, then makes her way out the door.

I sink into the squeaky vinyl of the guest chair. Rhythmic hospital quiet drops over the room—beeps and breaths, chatter and shuffles—but we're here in isolation.

I can't tell if Dad looks different than he did this past spring. Thinner and paler, obviously. His hair looks grayer. He's still the big man—as tall and wide as Dan—he's always been. I've always wondered if being larger than everyone around us puts us at a disadvantage. If perhaps it's more difficult for people to accept that a muscular man who towers over everyone might be in pain.

Even with the sedative, the pain radiates off Dad.

But then again, pain always radiates off my father.

Dad sighs again and rolls slightly. His hand flops onto the crinkly mattress. A deep, shallow groan echoes from his throat. The bed doesn't give him a lot of room.

"Gwen?" he mumbles.

It's been a decade. Ten years, and my dad still mumbles my mother's name.

I lean close to the bed. "Dad, it's Tom." Slowly, I place my hand on his arm.

He's like touching parchment. My father isn't old enough to feel as if he's going to crumble and blow away. Not at fifty-four. He's a moose, like me. There's too much of us to wither.

His eyes slowly open. "Sal said Rob should be here soon."

"Tomorrow, Dad." I look up at the clock. "They're going to kick me out in about twenty minutes."

Dad grunts. "It's that late?"

"They gave you a sedative. The nurse says you need to sleep."

The feeble light seeping in through the slats over the window catches in my dad's eyes and they spark like emeralds. We're an amalgam of our parents, Rob, Dan, and I. All three of us carry as much of our mom's baby blues as we do our dad's brilliant greens.

A feeble grin appears on Dad's lips, then vanishes just as fast. "Robert found himself a woman with spunk. Have you looked at her work? She's got the talent, I tell ya." He rolls onto his back. "I'm going to be a grandpa again."

"Sounds like it." Little Quidells everywhere.

Dad chuckles. "Have you eloped with your spunky one yet?" He chuckles again. "Don't let that one go." He waves a finger. "She'll keep you on track."

I lean back in the creaking chair. "She does."

Dad closes his eyes again. "They want me to go to Phoenix for tests."

I rub my face and my hand pushing down over my skin feels as if it's pushing rocks down my throat. "Tests?" No one said anything about driving to Phoenix for more tests. "Not Flagstaff?"

Flagstaff is a lot closer.

"It'll be okay, son." Dad sighs. "The doc came by this morning when they moved me into this room."

A person only gets so much time in the ICU. They probably moved him while I was on the airplane. "What did the doc say, Dad?"

"Nothing I didn't already know." He closes his eyes again.

I lean forward. "Dad?" But he doesn't open his eyes. "What did the doctor say?"

"That they want me to go to Phoenix for tests." His breathing settles.

He's asleep again.

I glance at the door. It's late. Is there someone around to give me real info?

My knees creak when I stand and I wobble just enough that my hand shoots out. I grip the rail on Dad's bed.

Like my dad, my legs are too obstinate to listen to reason—and to make life easy on the rest of me.

Dad snorts softly. I lean against his bed. Visiting hours are almost over.

I look down at Dad one last time before walking for the door. Why am I pouting like a little kid? This isn't about me.

The weight of the world is never personal.

Alma called the attending physician.

A blanketing feeling floods my brain, and for a split second the colors around me—the beiges and grays of the hospital hallway's walls, the flat, slightly-pink vinyl flooring under our feet, the doctor's yellowish-green scrubs—all brighten. All intensify. They take on the smothering and the unreality and the dream sense of being overwhelmed. They cease to be the colors within the space but reflections of the moment: The beiges and the grays take on the rolling depth of smoke and fog. The pinkish floor swims as if infected with killer algae. The doctor's scrubs become choking weeds.

And I wonder if *this* is the moment I dreamed of the night I started the painting.

I'm walking toward the doctor before he gets a greeting out of his mouth.

Military, I think. I don't know why. Maybe it's in how he stands. Maybe it's because he seems to be aware of his surroundings. He watches me with deep brown eyes and a take-no-shit gaze.

"Dr. Estafan Torre." He extends his hand. "You must be Thomas."

"Call me Tom. Please." We shake once.

Dr. Torre nods toward my dad's room. "The good news is that your father suffered only a partial blockage." His slight Mexican accent thickens. "The angioplasty opened the artery and his heart should be fine."

That take-no-shit look didn't loosen. If anything, the doctor's stance hardened.

"The bad news?" I ask.

Dr. Torre looks up at me. "He has a mass below his left lung, Mr. Quidell." He looks over my shoulder at Dad's room. "The best course of action is imaging and a biopsy."

Mass rockets around inside my head. The doctor's body language screams *I think it's malignant* even if he doesn't say it.

Mass and *biopsy* and *malignant*.

My dad's going to die.

Dr. Torre's stance shifts. "We've scheduled the appointments but he'll need someone to drive him to the clinic in Phoenix." He stares at my face as if to make sure I understand.

I see Sal round the corner and walk toward the room. "We'll take care of it."

The doctor looks back at Dad's room. "They will image and biopsy first. If it needs to come out, they will admit him into the Surgery Center. The surgeon there is your best option."

I nod. "Thank you, doctor."

He shakes my hand and walks away.

Sal watches the doctor go, but she looks at me as if she's seeing the same fog that consumed my father a decade ago threaten me.

She pats my arm. "Text your family."

Her words pull me from the hazy smothering of the moment. She's right. I have work to do, and that work will keep my brain busy. No more thinking about thick colors or concrete gullies.

I pull out my phone and walk toward the front of the hospital.

CHAPTER 17

Thomas

He didn't tell Sal he was sick. He didn't tell Rob or Dan or me, either. He didn't tell anyone.

The air cooled some after the sun went down but Sal told me to go in when she dropped me off at Dad's house. Said something about coyotes and mountain lions—predators—but I need the air. Real air, not conditioned air, or medicinal hospital air. So I found a lawn chair in Dad's garage and took up watch on his front walk.

He doesn't have food in his house, but he did have a six pack of marginal beer. It's not the handcrafted, artisanal stuff I'm used to. It's bitter and watery, but it will do.

I take a sip wishing he had vodka.

Though I've never liked the hard stuff. Beer and wine, and the occasional celebratory champagne for me. I don't like losing control.

I take another sip of the marginal beer.

The mountains ring the horizon like shadows of sharpened teeth. They're about to take a bite out of the distant sun and the indigo sky, the wispy, almost burgundy clouds, and the one-in-a-million shooting stars.

Somewhere nearby, an animal yips. It sounds vaguely dog-like, and I suspect it's one of Sal's coyotes. They're different down here, in the desert. The coyotes here have a lot less tolerance for humans than the urban animals around home.

They really are predators.

I take one last pull on my beer. Isa texted not long ago. They'd crossed into Sedona city limits and would be here within minutes.

Then I'll get to tell them the full details of my conversation with the attending physician. I could only text so much while they were driving.

The growl of Isa's crossover precedes the glare of the car's head-lights. They crawl down the lane, obviously looking closely at the houses. It's been a while since Rob's visited, as well, and I suspect in the dark, he doesn't quite remember which house it is.

The crossover pulls into the driveway. The engine dies and the lights go out. I blink, my eyes adjusting once again to the night, and I set my beer bottle on the concrete of the walk under my lawn chair.

I don't get up. I don't know why. I just don't. It's Rob, my younger brother, not the president. Just Rob and Isa.

Rob is small for a Quidell—he's close enough to six feet to claim it but Rob looks like a giant when he unfolds from the driver's seat.

He still carries the same chocolate brown tones in his black hair that Dan and I share, but he looks more like our mother than either of us. He is undoubtedly our father's most handsome son.

I used to give him crap about romancing girls all the time. He used to give me crap about drawing all the time. We fought a lot. Some-times, one of us would land a punch. Then Dan would send us to our rooms.

Now Rob's married and I'm the one following people around like a little kid.

My sister-in-law slowly unfurls from the passenger seat. She's in jeans and one of Rob's t-shirts and bright green flip flops. They slap against the concrete of the walk as she hurries toward me, a rhythmic *smack smack smack*. "Tom," she says, and bends over to give me a gentle hug.

I finally stand up. Rob's pulling luggage out of the car and I should help.

Isa squeezes my hand. "Sorry we didn't make visiting hours."

She's pale in the dim light thrown by my dad's porch light. Her blonde ponytail washes out her skin more than brightens her face, and I wonder how she's dealing with morning sickness on top of extra driving and a sick father-in-law.

I look her over. "You feeling okay? Still throwing up?"

Isa sticks her hands in her front pockets.

I almost say "It's temporary," but I figure I'd better keep my mouth shut. I left one angry woman back home. No need to anger another.

Isa frowns but flares her fingers over her belly. "It's not bad," she says, but it's obvious to me that she's lying.

My brother drops their bags on my lawn chair and throws his arms around my shoulders. "Thank you for flying down."

What else was I going to do? Dad needs us.

"Rob needs to be back at school in two weeks." Isa stretches her back. "He's planning on finishing out this year." She pats her belly. "We don't have a due date yet, but it's going to be close to spring finals."

Not long ago she was Rob's ex-girlfriend. Now she's his pregnant wife.

"The doctor only said he has a mass?" Rob picks up the bags again. "Dad never said anything about feeling sick."

I usher them into the house. "We need to take him to Phoenix for a follow-up."

Rob drops their bags on the same chair I dropped mine on earlier today. He steps to the side and rubs his shoulder like it hurts. "Okay. We'll get this under control. Get him checked out and healthy." He closes his eyes but the set of his mouth says he doesn't believe his own words.

Isa flips on the dining room light and her fingers immediately find the strap of the camera sitting next to my dad's laptop. It's an ornate, padded thing, but the beading and the designs are all in blacks, blues, and violets. Dad carries his camera around by hanging it from the shimmering night.

"Sammie wants me to update my online portfolio," Isa says absently.

Strands of her blonde hair have escaped from her ponytail and the crossed pins she uses to control it. Her skin does look pale, and under the harsh light over the table I see shadows under her eyes.

Isa has a knack for seeing the truth in people. Her ability erupts from her work like crackling electricity and I can only hope that I can paint as well as she photographs.

I don't want her in harm's way any more than Sammie. And the odd, vibrating sense I had back home, the feeling that something is *wrong*, resurfaces. Isa shouldn't be in the presence of a predator, either.

Or maybe I'm just reacting to the father I rarely see having a heart attack and...

I drop into one of the chairs surrounding the table. "He's fifty-four."

Isa walks toward the fridge. Rob drops into the chair next to mine. "Yeah," he says. "Yeah."

He watches Isa more than me. "Honey? Why don't you go to bed?"

They throw each other a series of looks that, I suspect, are a short-hand for something I don't understand, but Isa kisses Rob's cheek and makes her way toward the back of the house and the bedrooms.

"Take the master," I say. To Rob: "I don't need the big bed."

Isa nods over her shoulder and disappears into the hallway.

"I should bring in her equipment." Rob sounds just as absent as Isa.

I don't argue. I don't say anything. I think we're both too tired to talk about it right now.

And I don't think either of us wants to. "We'll go visit him tomorrow morning," I say.

Rob nods. He stands and squeezes my shoulder. I swear the absence I feel from him and Isa is the same energy—or lack thereof—in the air behind the glass door into Dad's hospital room.

"How's Sammie?" Rob asks.

When I look back at my brother, he's staring at my face in, I suspect, the same way I was just staring at him.

"Someone has to keep the job with the insurance," I say.

Rob shakes his head. Thankfully, he doesn't say anything.

But he does pat my arm. "Text her."

"I will." How else will I stay on track?

Rob stands. "Bed," he says, and walks away toward his wife, leaving me all alone out here in the dining room, under the harsh light permeating my father's house.

CHAPTER 18

Samantha

My phone rings and I shake fully awake in one jolting, earthquake-like moment. The phone rings again and I realize I'm not breathing.

Sun blasts through the gaps between the curtains. Road noise from outside vibrates the bed. Mickles meows and purrs and rubs his earthy-fluffy fur against my nose. Tom's t-shirt—the one I'm wearing and that he left on the bed before I took him to his brother's—bunches up under my back. The collar pulls on my throat.

My phone screams one more time.

Tom? I think. He's not in the bed with me and it takes me a moment to process why. He's supposed to be here. He's supposed to be happy and smiling and my anchor against my can-do attitude.

But he's wading into bad shit right now a thousand miles away.

I snatch the phone off the nightstand.

It's my boss. It's also ten o'clock.

"Oh my God I'll be there as soon as I can!" I groan as I drop my feet off the side of the bed. I'm never late. *Never*. What if Tony decides to lay me off, too?

Tony's a frowny man with a frowny face. His smiles always look forced, as does his hairline. He's too blocky to be round, and I think his body wants to morph itself into a fire hydrant and all the racquet-ball and golf in the world isn't going to stop it.

"You don't sound so good, Samantha." Tony calls me Samantha. He's formal that way. He calls everyone by the name their mom would use when yelling from the kitchen. "Samantha Miranda Singleton! I told you to clean your room *right now*, young lady!" Tony is everyone's stern parent.

I think he likes formal names because his is just Tony. Not Antony or Antoine, just plain old Tony.

He's not a bad boss. Just middle management. "Any news from Tom?" he asks.

The first thing I did yesterday was go into his office and tell him about Tom's dad, just in case. I didn't want to spring a surprise funeral on my boss.

I spent the rest of the day watching for the handful of texts I got from Tom. I think Isa and Rob sent me more information than my fiancé.

The doctors plan on releasing Jeremiah tomorrow. He gets a day at home and then they're taking him to Phoenix to get his lungs checked. Dan's flying in at the same time, so Rob will be picking him up while Tom waits at the hospital.

When I asked why the hospital didn't transfer him directly, Tom said something about insurance and "medically necessary transport."

I figured if the docs were okay with sending him home, then it must not be too bad.

"Nothing new," I say to Tony, still sitting on the edge of the bed. Still alone. Still... cold. Because that's what I am. Cold. Cold and feeling guilty.

"Are you sure *you're* okay?" He really does sound like the male version of my mom. "Missing meetings isn't like you."

No, it's not. I stare at my naked toes on the cold floor. Mickles meows and rubs against my side like the demanding, food-deprived kitty he is. "Why didn't you wake me up?" I whisper to the cat.

"I'm sorry, Tony." Why is the floor cold? It's still summer outside. "It won't happen again."

"Do you need to take a few days?"

Now? "We're in the middle of testing." *I don't want to get laid off*, I think.

"Samantha. Go be with your fiancé." A chair squeak echoes across the line. "It's fine. You did the planning last week. We can coast a few days without you."

I don't know what to say, other than "Don't lay me off," and a hard, small ball of tension rolls around in my gut. Is this what Tom's been feeling? I understood, but I didn't *really* understand.

And I'm suddenly confused.

That small ball jumps and pops. Tony says something else but I don't quite hear. I think the hairs on my arms want to stand on end but there's no reason to and they're just as confused as me.

My tension finds its way into my throat.

"Yeah, okay, Tony," I say. "You're right. Thank you."

The glare from outside looks too bright. Am I having a panic attack? Why would I be having a panic attack? I suck in my breath.

"Listen, Sam," he says, using Sam and not Samantha, like a mom trying to soothe. "Remember two years ago? When my wife's father passed?"

I nod, then realize he can't see me, and say, "Yeah."

"If this is the first time either of you have had to deal with something like this..." He pauses for a second. "Being laid off is hard enough. Then this. A lot can sneak up on you, okay? Just take care of yourself. I need my star in tip-top shape. How else will we dazzle the ad guys, huh?"

"Thanks, Tony."

"Let me know how you want to handle things this week. Use the network to grab any files you need if you want to work from home."

We talk about contingencies. My toes grow colder, exposed as they are. The ball of tension continues to bounce around inside my chest like an old-school video game.

Beep bop. Beep bop.

I set the phone on the blankets. The bedroom swims in shadows and all I want to do is fling open the curtains. Let in the heat and the light and make all the bad things scurry away.

Mickles forces his way onto my lap. He stands on my thighs and presses the great existential truth of cats down into my flesh—*I may be little, but I am fierce.*

"You're going to leave bruises if you continue to press so hard, my dear Mr. Pickles."

He meows and purrs, obviously looking more for food than affection. I glance at my phone. No new texts from Tom, but it's still early in Arizona.

I wonder if I should just go back to bed.

No. I can work while I wait. At the very least, the studio needs cleaning. I rub at my belly and the t-shirt. It's Tom's, the same 90s concert t-shirt I wore the morning after he first brought me home.

He'd been fiercely unapologetic about wanting to be with me. About being willing to fight to make sure I felt whole and safe.

It was immediate for us. Love at first sight. Shit like that's not supposed to happen but damn it, sometimes the universe doesn't want to wait around for you to figure out what needs figuring. Tom helped me understand why I needed to leave a terrible boyfriend, and moved me into his place, and I don't ever want to be apart from him again.

Some of us are just lucky, I guess. I lucked out with Tom. At least I'm smart enough to realize it.

I pluck at the t-shirt. Like all of Tom's clothes, I'm swimming inside it. But it smells like him, warm, bright, and complex, like art. I'd cocoon myself in the shirt for the rest of my days if I could.

I pull the fabric to my face and inhale deeply. *Tom* fills my soul and I almost feel him. Almost sense the touch of his fingers along the skin of my shoulders. Almost feel his palm on my breast and his breath on my neck. I almost see his smile and the perfection of his blue-green eyes.

I almost drown inside missing him.

This is the first time we've been apart like this. The first time one of us left angry and with no promise of a return.

Why did I have to argue with him? Why didn't I see his pain? I sniff at the shirt again. Why didn't I smell it on him?

I flop onto the mattress. Mickles meows his displeasure. Above my head, open beams cross the ceiling and pierce the walls, and continue on into the bathroom, hallway, and open areas of the loft. Shadows lurk up there.

"That's it." I slap the blanket. I might not be able to directly help Tom or his family, but I can still rep his work. Hell, I can babysit Bart, if that's what's needed.

My phone rings, but this time, it's not Tony.

Or Tom.

"Juri," I say, doing my best to sound professional. "I was expecting a call from Barb."

He laughs. "Barb's moving on." I hear mumbles. Someone else must be in the room with him. "I'm looking for a new assistant."

The small ball of tension in my gut explodes. Is Juri offering me a job? One with much better pay and a lot smaller chance of getting laid off?

"Sam, listen," he says, "I'm at the Vegas property. Flew in last night." More mumbling behind him. His voice lowers. "It's a fucking mess." I hear what sounds like glass rattling. "I could use a fresh pair of eyes."

My brain should be making all sorts of contingency plans. I should be formulating questions and answers. But all I can think is *Oh my God*.

"So, Samantha Singleton, do you want to give me a hand?"

CHAPTER 19

Thomas

"Look at this." Rob hands me yet another official-looking piece of paper. "The Sedona Arts Council commissioned three works last year."

I take the paper from his hand. He's not looking at me. He's scowling at the mess in front of him.

We spent the entire day at the hospital working out the specifics of Dad's Phoenix visit. How much walking he can do, and the generals of moving around, about snacks and hydration and breaks. Hotel rooms have been booked. Sal's on notice. Rob will go to the airport and pick up Dan—assuming he doesn't develop a fever between now and then—while Isa and I wait out the biopsy.

Then we deal with what needs to be dealt with.

After all the tests, unless we run into something catastrophic, Rob and Isa will be leaving for Los Angeles from Phoenix. Dan and I will bring Dad home once the doctors have a plan.

If it is cancer and it's operable, they'll take it out right away. If it's not operable, they'll get a plan in place and send him home. The doctors say they can handle chemo here.

If it's benign, then it's a slightly different surgery—I didn't catch the specifics—and we can all go home happy and healthy after a few days of recovery.

The sun went down hours ago. Rob, Isa, and I should have gone to bed the moment we returned to the house. I'm exhausted. Rob is, too. And Isa should be taking it easy. But Rob walked out of Dad's office with files, instead. We dumped it out onto the dining room table, next to his laptop.

Dad's "system" consists of a yearly banker's box. Everything goes into the box. Every notice, every receipt, big or small. Business-related, house-related, car-related—they're all in the box. We've already found a full mound of grocery receipts, plus paper copies of all his utility bills. Materials receipts are also scattered throughout the mess. Rob and I haven't even yet dared to open his home and business accounts software.

And now Rob's found documentation of a commission.

"He never said anything about this." I take the paper. It's thick, heavy bond and linen-feeling, with an embossed Council seal.

Isa pokes her head out of the kitchen. "I asked him point-blank if he had any shows coming up." She sets down the bottle of spices she found in the cupboard. "When Rob set up for us to see your gallery show, Tom."

"He probably didn't want to be a distraction." Though I doubt Rob and Isa believe that any more than I do.

"We need to grocery shop tomorrow." She taps the top of the reddish-looking spices.

"What's he been living on?" Rob pushes aside a couple more papers. "Mom's Social Security." He pushes another paper. "Odd jobs." He looks up. "I swear, he's never said anything."

"I don't think he's talked to Dan, either." I point at the paper. "He got a little from this." Not a lot, but enough to probably get him through a couple of months.

But that was a year ago.

Isa walks over and kisses Rob's cheek. "I'm going to bed."

He squeezes her hand. "I'll be there in a bit."

She kisses him again and walks toward the master bedroom.

Rob shuffles more papers. "Isa and I can't stay more than a few days." He sits back in his chair. "We need to get our insurance settled. I need to be back at school before classes start. I'm teaching."

Like Dan, Rob is an employed man. I sip at my water. "I can query editors from here as easily as I can from home."

Rob looks relieved. He blinks and rubs at his cheek. "My eyes are starting to blur."

I chuckle. "Yeah."

He neatens up a stack. Not that it really matters. Like me, he sips his water, and we sit in silence. Isa moves around in the bathroom. The faucet in the kitchen drips. Outside, a coyote howls. And my brother and I wonder in tandem about life.

Rob slaps the table. "Time to snuggle with my pregnant wife."

Finally, something that makes me smile. "I can't believe you got married first."

"Dan said exactly the same thing." Rob stands and stretches his back. "Guess I can't be the immature one anymore, huh?"

"You were never as immature as you pretended to be."

Rob walks toward the hall leading into the bedrooms, but stops. "Yes, I was," he says, and walks away into the back rooms of my father's little house.

I look at the commission paperwork again. The deadline is coming up.

Dad's studio is behind the house, down a covered walk that snakes around the patio. It used to be a shed of some kind; it's small but it opens to the mountain breezes. When the heat gets to be too much, he has a window air conditioner unit that looks as old as me.

Like most houses here, a wall circles the entire yard. In some places, it's head-high concrete block. In others, waist-high wrought iron. Dad's painted it in motifs reminiscent of local rock art.

I haven't gone out to his studio yet. I don't want to pry. But if he's been working on the commission, I should check on it. At least make sure his studio is secure. It's not like he'd share with me if he needed anything.

Or like I'd ask.

I grab the studio key off its hook next to the patio and throw open the door. The dry Arizona heat slaps me full force even though the land is now fully blanketed by night. The mountains circling the horizon look like the absence of teeth. Negative space has come to bite into the brilliant stars above.

The coyote I heard earlier howls again, so I peer into the gloom, to make sure I'm alone.

I swear I see a set of yellow eyes staring at me through two iron posts. Something shuffles beyond the concrete garden wall, and something else skitters. A low *yip* follows, then quiet. Whatever watched me through the fence must have decided I'm not worth its time.

I grab the baseball bat leaning against the wall just outside the door anyway.

Small, scruffy trees grow along the fence. A couple of large prickly pear cactuses sprawl unkempt in the corner. The patio extends about halfway to the fence, and the walk to the studio breaks up the uneven, hole-ridden dirt ground.

At the edge of the patio, I stop and listen. No more coyote noises yap through the still air, only the constant hum of many, many AC units. Inside, Isa laughs. Shadows move by their window. The light goes out. Tonight, my brother snuggles with his wife.

And I suddenly feel the full stillness of the air. The heat crawls along my skin and my body can't decide if it likes it or not.

I miss Sammie's touch.

I left under not-so-good circumstances. I made her feel as if I don't trust her. I do. I know I do, all the way to my bones. Yet I can't shake the feeling that this shit storm has two fronts.

Dad's studio stands in the far corner of the yard, a dark, low box with an adobe roof. Shadows hide its blue exterior, but I pick out hints of sky, and water, and the aurora borealis over snow.

You can take the artist out of the frozen north, but you can't take the frozen north out of the artist.

I press the key into the lock. Tumblers roll, metal clicks, and the door creaks open. I flip on the lights.

My childhood opens up before me.

Dad set up his Arizona studio to look exactly like his studio in the house where I grew up. High windows circle the roof line—they're shaded to block direct sunlight, but the space is probably flooded with indirect sunlight during the day—just like at home. One wall is bright white, also like home. I used to tape paper to that wall—not the wall in front of me, but his studio wall when he was... still with us. Before he disappeared from our lives, in soul and later in body.

I'd position the paper *just so*, and spend the entire day with him. He'd paint. I'd paint. He'd draw. I'd draw. He never sent me away.

Seven, maybe eight canvases lean against the wall next to the door. The one on top feels eerie and dark—purples and greens swirl around a figure of a woman, but it's not even halfway finished. The one behind it carries only a splash of black paint; the next one is blank.

The last three scream from the shadows. One erupts with the colors I associate with the Southwest, one the colors of the world he left behind. The third, a blend. They're abstracts... but not.

A ghost haunts each piece. The same ghost painted with the same colors and the same strokes. She floats through the long path of these three paintings, burning with fire and ice. I look at the purple and green figure of the first painting. It's the same ghost. The same icy, burning woman. Hints of blood dot the swirls around her, so faint, so specific, they're texture, not shape or color.

And there, under the arm of the first ghost, is a second, smaller woman.

I drop the canvases against the wall. I understand what the painting is—I feel it in my fingers as much as I do my soul. This is how Dad processes pain. This savage, open-wound way.

But I can't look at the gash in his soul, not when he's in a hospital bed. I can't.

I turn off the light, lock the door, and walk back to the house, bat in hand. The coyote leaves me be, probably out of respect. I close and lock the patio door.

Rob and Isa's bed bounces against the wall of their bedroom. Each little thump echoes through my father's hollow house. I just stare at the moonlight playing over the mess of papers on the table.

I don't know if I will show Rob the paintings in Dad's studio. I'm not sure he needs to see that, not with a baby on the way. He processed Mom and Jeanie's deaths a long time ago. He did his time in therapy. He doesn't need to see their ghosts.

I walk down the hall toward the guest room, ready to spend the rest of the night alone inside my dad's world.

CHAPTER 20

Thomas

I stop walking just outside the shadow thrown by the covered drop-off area in front of the hospital's entrance. The noises of civilization flutter through the dry, warm air: Road noise. The entrance door swishing open. Isa speaking to Dad in hushed tones by the entrance, where they wait. Rob as he whistles his way toward the parking lot.

It's time to take Dad home.

The pavement is hot in front of Sedona's small hospital, out here in the open and without shade. The heat feels nice this morning, sort of like a full-body therma-wrap after a difficult workout. It's a relief seeing Dad with some color in his cheeks, and Rob confident that the Phoenix doctors will mop up what needs mopping so we all can get on with our lives.

But the bright, midmorning sun dances along my phone and I squint at the screen.

I'm on my way to Vegas, Sammie's text says.

Fuck, I think. Just one, all-purpose swear word. That's it. Not *What the fuck?* Or *Why?* Or *I thought we talked about this.* Just one lone *Fuck* as if that simple monosyllable effectively sums up my entire life.

Call me after you get your dad settled, the next text says. *I want to go over the game plan with you once I land.*

I still feel like I need to get Dad's baseball bat and drive to Vegas *right now,* because my gut's telling me that Sammie's about to fly into a fucking den of coyotes.

But I can't. Dad needs me. Rob and Isa need me. Like Dan, they have work. They can't camp out in Sedona.

Will do, I text back. *We're taking him home right now.*

Love you, appears on my screen and for a moment, I feel as if I'm allowed to set down the weights that are making my muscles cramp. Sammie handed me water and I drink it in, but the weight—the rocks and the masses—I can't be left out here in the parking lot, under the sun. I need to pick them up again.

Love you, too, I text.

A new shadow falls over my screen. Rob walked back from the car and now watches me from behind his sunglasses, his eyes shaded too much for me to tell if he's concerned or annoyed.

"Sammie's flying to Las Vegas. She thinks she can set up a deal with Olson Companies for Isa and me."

A satisfied nod tips Rob's head toward Isa and Dad behind me, where they wait in front of the hospital exit. "Did you hear that?" he asks.

She shades her eyes and asks Dad a question. He shields his eyes as he looks up at her from his wheelchair. Even along the covered drive, sunlight bounces around and adds a squint-inducing glare to the world.

"It's too bright out here to hear anything," she says.

Rob chuckles and walks toward the parking lot and the crossover. "Best not to argue with the pregnant woman," he calls.

I should laugh. I should agree and not be so... what? Rigid? No, it's not that. Gloomy? Maybe.

Dad watches my attention flicker between him, Rob, Isa, and my phone. He looks comfortable and uncomfortable at the same time— we brought him sweats to wear for the trip home, but his big frame is wedged into the metal and blue vinyl of the wheelchair.

Like me. The day's heat warms my aches but I'm wedged into a place I don't want to be.

Maybe I'm just a bullheaded Quidell. You'd think we would have collectively learned our lesson by now but no, here I am under a cloud of frustration with my girlfriend while carrying the sharp, cutting remnants of my father's broken heart.

I wave to Isa and Dad, and jog after Rob. "I don't like Sammie flying to Vegas without back-up," I say.

Rob holds out the key fob and hits *unlock*. Two aisles away, the crossover beeps and clicks. "Why?" No eye roll or *humph* from my brother, for which I'm grateful. He only glances at me as we part and walk around a car, him to the right, toward the nose of the crossover and the driver's side, and me to the left, toward the passenger's side.

"Bad feelings." Because that's what it is. Bad feelings. Bad dreams and abandoned paintings. Mine. Dad's. Lost jobs and lost directions. Ethereal New Age mumbo jumbo.

I stop next to the crossover's door. Rob stops on the other side of the car. Neither of us touches the exterior.

Rob pulls off his sunglasses. "Don't push Sammie away the way Dan pushed Camille away when he felt overwhelmed, okay? Stoic man-against-the-world only works when it's you versus bears and boulders." He tucks the temple of his glasses over the collar of his t-shirt. "The ladies be formidable."

I chuckle. "Formidable is good."

Rob gingerly pats the car roof. "Sammie can take care of herself. Her job is to take care of the commission part of your career." He points at Isa. "That's what we're all paying her the big bucks for, correct?"

I nod.

"Let her do her job." He pulls open his door.

"Yeah." But my brain keeps whispering *Predators! Coyotes!* Stalking and death.

I don't say anything. Rob will only call me melodramatic. Hell, when Dan had his pigheaded moment with Camille, both Rob and I called *him* melodramatic. But neither of us understood that Dan has scars that had healed wrong. Scars that made parts of his life that should be able to take a kick so tender that the lightest brush had our ex-firefighter brother on the ground in pain.

I duck into the car. Rob focuses more on getting us through the lot and to the pick-up than chatting about formidable ladies, and cuts the engine when we pull up in front of Dad and Isa.

I push myself out of the passenger seat, to make room for Dad.

Isa holds up her phone. "Vegas, baby!" Her phone beeps and she scrolls. "This could be huge, Tom."

Isa seems happy. She holds her phone out for Dad to see. "Sammie's got a major lead for Tom and me."

Dad tips his head as if he's looking over the top of a pair of non-existent glasses and squints at the screen. "I should have had you bring me my reading glasses."

Isa pats his shoulder. When he looks up at her, she gives him a quick hug. "We'll get you fixed up so you can come to Vegas and see our first show."

My father's face falls. His cheeks sag more than they had before, and I swear the shadows under his eyes darken. The look winks by so fast I'm sure neither Isa nor Rob caught it.

He thinks he's going to die, erupts in my head. Not a scream, not a yell, the thought manifests itself in the full visual-metaphor glory of wispy, bloody, dark ghosts. As the muddy reds and violets of fear. It's an overlay on the real world, one that turns the edges where my dad's form overlaps the inanimate hospital background into ragged, sawing boundaries.

Lines turn into traps and my artist's brain sees the unreal clarity of just exactly what my dad's expression means.

Isa takes Rob's hand when he walks up. "I need to get back to the studio. Get the paperwork under control." She glances over her shoulder and smiles at me as if to say *Don't worry*.

So I push it down. Push aside the sharp and jagged shards of my father's problems.

Isa frowns a little, then quickly leans her head against Rob's shoulder. Slowly, Dad lifts his weight out of the wheelchair. He teeters slightly, but Rob has his arm.

Dad grins and pats his son's hand. "I'm alright."

He's lying erupts. The jaggedness of my father's edges takes on a veiled hollowness. The truth is in there somewhere, but it's smothered under layers of denial and the shrouds left by ghosts.

Rob and I help him into the car. Dad leans his head against the headrest and we wait for Isa to return from wheeling his chair back into the reception area.

"Your mother would have liked her." He nods in Isa's general direction, then twists his head toward me. "Sammie, too."

Rob shrugs. Dad's comment isn't abnormal. Not to him. But for me, it makes the *He thinks he's going to die* thought harden into a crystalline hunk of granite. The wind's not going to blow away this one.

I duck into the cramped back seat.

Isa scoots in next to me. "Doctor said you can have hot sauce on your scrambled eggs, Jeremiah." She pats Dad's shoulder. "But not *too* much."

Dad grins and pulls his seatbelt across his lap. "None of that crap bottled in China." He points out the window. "Live off the land. That's what I say."

Isa laughs and Rob starts the car. We make our way through the streets of Sedona. The afternoon sun shines down on the crossover and the concrete. The mountains glow. Scrub trees flitter in the breeze, and every so often, a dog barks at our passing car.

And I wonder about predators and ghosts. And about the many ways to die.

But I don't want to think about grays and blacks laced with subtle reds. I don't want my mind to clamp down on the textures of dried blood when I'm surrounded by the newness of what should be an appreciated future.

The mass isn't that big. It might be benign. And like Rob said, Sammie can take care of herself.

But still, malignant predators lurk. Dad might be right about dying. And Sammie might be about to offer up herself—and Isa and me—to something just as writhing and vicious.

Or I'm fucking overreacting.

But first, we settle Dad. No need to worry until all biopsies come back, both from Phoenix and from Las Vegas.

CHAPTER 21

Samantha

McCarran International Airport is still the chrome and glitz expanse it was the last time I stepped foot in Las Vegas. Still hot and dry. Still full of international tourists and slot machines.

The giant, concrete scorpion at the base of the escalators is still weird and wonderful.

Maybe I'll come home from this trip with a commission for Tom that's just as weird and just as wonderful.

I can hope.

The hospital in Sedona is sending Tom's father home today. He's to report to the hospital in Phoenix on Friday. Dan timed his flight so that Tom can pick him up at the airport, though from Camille's last text, it sounds like Dan might be holding off a fever by the sheer force of his will.

Tom's calls have been subdued. He's been particularly vague about what the doctors have to say, and about how his father is doing, but I hear the same harshness in his voice I heard right before he left. The same pain.

So I'm going to make this work. I'm going to give him and his family something positive to focus on, and, perhaps, a positive for his father, too.

A driver in a classic black chauffeur uniform complete with hat and tie waits next to the baggage claim. The blocky, bright-red Olson Companies logo fills the backside of his sign, and when he sees my knot of passengers stepping off the escalator, he flips it over and holds up his cardboard square.

"Singleton," it says.

Juri sent a limo. I can't say I'm unhappy about it—the fewer days I need to rent a car, the cheaper this trip will be—but it makes me uneasy. Am I afraid of Juri's expectations? I can't help but wonder if he's romancing me, and not just potential employee romancing. That he sent a limo because of Vegas clichés.

I have this trip under control—it's fact-finding. Nothing else. What, exactly, does Juri have to offer? Once intelligence is gathered, I'll rent a car, drive to Sedona, and deliver good news.

No one needs to deal with extra what-ifs right now, so until that news becomes genuinely good, I'll keep the worrying to myself.

The driver is a tall, nicely built man—his shoulders are wider than his waist, but not too much so. He looks to me to be in his mid- to late-twenties, like me. His strong jaw, high cheekbones, and dark brown eyes suggest Japanese ancestry, but he has an ethnically-indeterminate look to him, which makes his already handsome face even more interesting. The formality of how he holds his body suggests he's serious about his job. When I approach, he smiles a disarming, handsome smile.

"Ms. Singleton?" He holds out his hand.

We shake. His grip is firm but not dominant, as if he understands how to use body language to say "professional" and "supportive" without opening up too much space for a client to take advantage.

I'm impressed. "Hello," I say.

"Remy Yoshida." Remy nods once and sweeps his arm toward the luggage carousel. "Welcome to Las Vegas, Ms. Singleton."

The bell shrieks. I luck out in that my bag is one of the first off the plane. Remy takes a moment to call into the office and let Juri's local assistant know that I've arrived safely. There's a lot of nodding and smiling. Remy's definitely good with customer service.

He opens a path through the crowd and we make our way to the special covered limo parking area just outside the main terminal.

"You are here to help with the new hotel?" he asks. I get the impression that Mr. Yoshida knows a lot more about the local operations of the Olson Companies than a "mere" chauffeur would.

"I represent two new up-and-coming artists whose work may be exactly what the new venture needs." Tom was right; I sound like a brochure. But if that's how I need to talk, then that's how I will talk.

Remy grins. He pulls a fob from his pocket and the full-size sedan of a limo in front of us beeps. Huge and black with fully-tinted windows, it actually looks just like all the other limos parked around it.

Remy takes my bag and pops open the trunk. "I'll be dropping you at The Imperial Sands, so you can settle into your room."

The Imperial Sands is the Olson Companies' five-star hotel located just off the Strip. The new property is located on the "redevelopment" end of the Strip proper and is adjacent to The Imperial Sands. My guess is that Juri is looking into ways to rehab the "historic" new property while connecting it to the already functioning hotel.

A connecting concourse would be an excellent location for a gallery. Vegas is full of such concourses—it's not difficult to move the entire length of the Strip without setting foot out in the heat. I wouldn't be surprised if the two properties were already connected.

I crawl into the limo. "Thank you," I say.

Remy closes my door and makes his way around to the driver's seat. "Sarah—one of Mr. Olson's assistants—will text you with—"

My phone trills.

Remy smiles and starts up the limo. "—dinner plans."

It's not Juri's assistant. It's Tom.

We have Dad home, his text says. *He's resting.*

You rest too, I respond. I can't help that I worry. *I'm on the way to my hotel. I promise not to gamble away our life savings.*

Thank you appears. That's it. No joking response. Just *Thank you.*

He's more worried than he's letting on.

I'll take pictures of the gallery space, I text. *Tell Isa I'll let you know when*

I meet with Juri. I want him to know that no secrets will be kept. *I'd like to introduce you both.*

I also want Juri to know.

Okay. Great. What time?

A new beep signals the appearance of Assistant Sarah's text. I forward the entire exchange to Tom and by the time Remy pulls up in front of The Imperial Sands, he seems to be handling the whole affair better. His responses come in faster.

"Here you are, Ms. Singleton." Remy hands me his card at the same time he hands over my bag. "If you need anything—tickets, a ride, reservations—please call. I'm at your service." He bows once and ushers me toward the wide, gilded doors of Juri Olson's Las Vegas property.

"Thank you, Remy." I stuff the card into my pocket. "I will."

He returns to his limo. I turn toward the grand Roman columns and the heat-tortured potted palms. The noises of the Strip filter in between the twenty-story hotels and the rushing buses and trucks. People laugh. Attractions whoosh and chime. Barkers yell out entice-ments to gamble away that life savings your fiancé so kindly asked you to protect.

This is the Vegas the entertainment complex wants the tourists to see. But that's not why I'm here. I'm much more interested in the complex itself.

I wheel my bag toward the shimmering glass doors of the Olson Companies' soon-to-be-second-tier attraction, hoping that I can get us up onto the top shelf.

CHAPTER 22

Samantha

Like all hotels in Las Vegas, the Imperial Sands is home to several world-class restaurants. When we dated, Juri liked to brag about how he would poach chefs from famous places in New York, Chicago, even London and Paris, and bring them into his holdings. He said they like Vegas. Something about how it's easier to keep the wall up between their private life and their work life here.

It didn't make sense to me then, and it doesn't now. Workaholics will work themselves to death no matter where they live.

I will say, though, that whoever he poached for the Imperial Sands was worth the time and money.

"This is excellent." I take another bite of my perfectly-grilled filet mignon.

The savory aroma of the steak carries slight hints of sea salt. The potatoes, an undernote of garlic. Warmth all but wafts off the bread.

When Juri rattled off the long French name of the wine, I knew I was in for a treat.

Juri grins, and with wine glass in hand, sits back in his utterly comfortable, soft and luxurious, high-backed chair. The restaurant seated us in a cushy corner and now we both rest in velveteen uphol-stery so plush it shimmers with the same layered, rich burgundies as the wine.

I point at his chair, then mine. "How much does it cost to keep the seating clean?" The nightly upkeep on this place had to be more than my monthly salary.

Juri laughs. The nondescript, calming music of some random string quartet flows through the dining space. A few tables away, a woman laughs. The place is packed tonight, but it doesn't feel crowded. The tables sit at what I suspect are specific angles and placements to produce the correct ambiance while still maximizing the restaurant's profits.

"It's a classy joint." He raises his glass high and his auburn eyes sparkle. "We only let in classy people with good manners."

I laugh, but wave my fork at the walls. "I can help you with the boring art." It's all Renaissance still lifes and veiled women drawing water from wells.

Juri takes a sip of the French wine with the long-winded name. He holds the glass in front of his perfectly-tailored crisp white shirt, and gently swirls the liquid inside. "We should probably stay away from edgy nudes in the dining room."

I set down my fork. Of course Juri would drop a semi-innocuous comment about Tom's many paintings of me. But I don't think he's jabbing. His mouth isn't twisted in the slight smirk he tends to make when he tries to make someone squirm.

I think he's testing.

I pick up my fork again. "Photographs," I say. "Black and whites would give the space a hipper, more European feel. Patrons will feel..." I pause, trying to find the correct wording for what I want to say.

"Younger?" Juri offers. He sets his glass on the table and leans forward.

He's still testing me. "Not necessarily *younger*," I say, and snap my fingers. "Worldly. Eating here becomes part of the adventure."

Juri nods and slowly pushes the remains of his potato around his plate. "The corridor expansion between the Imperial Sands East and the new Imperial Sands West will house the world." He flicks his fingers through the air. "Points of connection, not just to places, but also to movements."

He sits back again. "Festivals. Nature. Inspiration."

All this in Las Vegas? "Here?" Now I wave my hand through the air.

Juri picks up his glass again. "There's the other property I haven't shown you yet." He winks.

"You want to hook them young, don't you?" I pick up my wine and swirl it, imitating Juri's semi-smug posture. "Offer environments where they can make rich and inspiring memories. Olson Companies wants to be your vacation-destination agent."

Juri raises his glass and winks again.

I was right. I pegged his game plan from the beginning. "We can help you with that."

He taps his finger on the table. "*You* can help me with that, Sam."

"Of course I can." I stuff another piece of steak in my mouth to give myself a moment to think. Is he offering me a job? Is he trying to bed me? Both?

Reading Juri shouldn't be this difficult.

"With Barb leaving, I'm down an executive assistant," he says.

I set down my fork and do my best to look annoyed, because I *am* annoyed. Did I go through all this just to have him offer me a job I'm not suited for so he can keep me close? It reeks of old-school boy's club bullshit.

"I'm a communications manager, not an office manager, Juri."

He laughs again. "Oh, I know." He finishes his wine and sets the glass next to his bread plate. "You are destined for a directorship." He tips his head back and peers at me over his nose. "Or an assistant vice president position."

With the Olson Companies? I think. "Are you offering me a job, Juri Olson?"

He taps the table again. "I need someone with vision to keep the designers and contractors on the same page." He nods as if he's just convinced himself that he's correct to offer me work. "I knew five years ago that you were destined for great things."

I feel warm. My heart races. My adrenaline crests and it takes effort not to jump up and dance around the restaurant.

I have the upper hand.

"So our time together was a scouting run, huh?" I smirk. I refuse to allow him to poke at our history just as much as I refuse to allow him to poke at my modeling.

He shrugs but his voice drops low. "An enjoyable scouting run, Sam."

I shake my head. "You are still a flirt, Juri." Best to call him on his behaviors.

Juri laughs. "I apologize if I've made you uncomfortable." He flicks a finger toward the restaurant's lavish view of the Strip. "I have no doubt you can handle the boys here."

Now I lean back. "Sounds as if I need to run a workshop on what is acceptable and what is not acceptable behavior from Olson Companies subcontractors."

A hearty guffaw rolls from Juri and he slaps the table. "Yes! I wish to keep my talent on staff."

I chuckle. "How much time will I need to spend here?" An unending stream of questions runs through my head: How much travel? What salary are you offering? Maybe we can pay off the loft sooner than we thought.

Juri leans forward. "Only the time you deem necessary."

"So no relocating?"

"Only if you want to." He sits back. "Your fiancé's father lives in Sedona, does he not? Maybe Tom would like to be closer to his dad."

I'm not sure if I'm shocked by Juri's research, or pissed off. But it does feel like yet another type of poking.

Juri grins and taps his finger on the table. "I did a search. Turns out there are two Quidell artists." He shrugs.

I still frown—and continue to wonder if he's pushing buttons and testing limits as part of the interview.

The formal interview—if I get to a formal interview—will have all the necessary formality. There will be questions about strengths and weaknesses, about work history and "where I see myself in five years."

But, I think, Juri is looking for fortitude. I set both my hands on the table. "I think I would like to see this other new property of yours, Juri Olson."

His grin looks almost shark-like.

For a split second, Tom's words about predators resurfaces, but I don't think Juri wants to take a bite out of me.

I think he wants me to join his hunt.

I pull out my phone. "I assume you have photos?" I wave it at him. "Let me share them with my talent. Get you those fresh eyes you so want."

Juri chuckles and pulls out his own phone. "The Foundation—it's an arts non-profit funded by my father—is setting aside a considerable pot for commissions, but they need guidance."

I'm not surprised the Olson family is playing the profit-non-profit game. Less commercial that way, plus they get a hefty tax write-off.

A link to a URL pops up on my phone. "I'll forward this," I say.

"Sam."

I look up. The shark look is gone, but what's replacing it looks worse. Not dangerous worse, but crestfallen worse. And the worst part of the worse is that I'm not sure if Juri means his expression to be empathetic, or if this is still a test.

"There are rules." He points at my phone. "Employees, family members, what not."

The frown on his face sure screams *test* to me.

"So sayeth the Foundation."

So that's it. Juri just handed me the ultimate test: Me or Tom. It's one or the other.

A job or a million-dollar commission.

CHAPTER 23

Thomas

Rob stuffs bagged spinach into Dad's fridge. "You know, maybe we should have stuck with shelf-stable." He tosses in a bag of carrots. "Seriously."

In his little living room on the other side of the dining room table, Dad pats at the blanket covering his legs and stretches himself out along the couch. "I'll make stew."

I don't think he's in any mood—or shape—to make stew. Neither am I. My neck hurts and I rub at it absently.

"The food will be fine until we get back from Phoenix." I set a loaf of bread on the counter. Everything we bought should be good until Dan and I return with Dad. Between the three of us, it won't last long, anyway.

"Did you buy my cookies?" Dad calls.

Rob holds up a new box of snickerdoodles. "Right here."

Isa scoops up the box and walks from the kitchen, behind me where I sit at the table, and toward Dad, who fusses over the pillow behind his back until Isa leans over him.

"Here, Jeremiah, let me." She hands him the box and makes quick work of arranging the couch, and Dad looks, finally, at least somewhat comfortable.

"It's a girl." Dad points at her belly after he sets the box on the coffee table. "She's going to look just like you."

Isa smiles and pats his shoulder. "I was hoping it was a boy. The only name we have picked out is Jeremiah."

Dad wiggles again, but this time I think it's because he's annoyed by Rob and Isa thinking about naming a grandbaby after him.

"No Jerry, okay?" He flicks on the television.

Isa pats his shoulder again. "I promise. No kids named Jerry."

Dad sits back, content for the moment to scan through the Netflix menus.

Isa returns to fiddling with her online portfolio as we wait for Sammie's text to "join in the fun."

At least she's doing something interesting. The receipts spread between my spot at the table and Dad's laptop look like a blizzard of brain-numbing numbers and letters.

I'd rather be staring at a blank canvas than dealing with the nitty-gritty of making it through the day.

"Tom will make the stew." Isa taps and clicks at her website. "Then freeze it in Quidell-man-sized single servings." She smirks at Rob.

"Hey!" Rob closes the fridge, waves his hand up and down in front of his body, and twists his hips to the side. "I work hard to maintain my girlish figure."

It's nice that they're joking around. It relieves tension.

"I know, sweetie." Isa makes kissy-lips at Rob.

It's been a long day, but Dad's home and resting. I glance over at him as he starts up some uproarious British sitcom. He chuckles, but I can't shake the sense of *He's going to die.*

I rub my neck again and stretch my shoulder. How did the aches sneak up on me like this? This is what I get for not exercising for a week.

Isa frowns. "I think you need to work out some of that tension."

Rob loads the last of the food into a cupboard. "Go for a run. We're good here. It's fine." He nods toward the door.

"Sammie's supposed to call." I can't leave.

Isa opens her mouth to say something, but both her phone and mine beep at the same time. *Juri gave me a URL.* A web address appears. *He wants to leverage the optics of this location.*

Isa shows the text to Rob, then taps away at her laptop. The site pops up. It's wide open, empty, and glorious. It looks more like a national park than a vacant lot in Las Vegas.

"Oh, wow," Isa says. She immediately starts conversing with Sammie.

"Who 'leverages the optics' of nature?" I grumble.

Rob chuckles.

I have it under control, pops up on my phone. *I think you're going to be happy.*

Probably not, I think. Not if my optics get leveraged. "What if Juri Olson wants to talk to us?"

"Isa can handle it," Dad calls. He chuckles again at the British antics on the screen.

Right now, sitting on the couch, he seems okay. The lighting in the house has given him back some of his color. He's agreeable, and happy.

In the chair next to me, a woman who knows a lot more about setting up productions and wrangling money men than I do scrolls through texts from my fiancé. She concentrates on the info appearing. Nothing about her stance says that she's upset about what she sees.

Isa waves her phone. "Sammie says she won't have any more information until tomorrow."

Rob pats my shoulder. "Go on." He points at the door again. "Be the aloof artist. Make Mr. Juri Olson understand that he's not worthy of talking to you directly."

Isa scowls at him. "Yet he can speak to *me?*"

Rob kisses her cheek. "You're the photographer from L.A. You know how to talk to people like Juri Olson. My bro here's a feral kid."

Isa continues to scowl, but she looks up at me. "It *would* be better if you didn't full-on growl at the man who might make us all rich." Then she returns her attention to her phone and taps something to Sammie. "Take your phone."

Of course I'll take my phone. I must have groaned or something because Rob slaps my shoulder and gives me a brotherly side-eye.

"What?" I ask.

Rob rolls his eyes and pushes me toward the door.

I point at the receipts. "Busy."

My phone chimes. *Go for a run* appears.

Isa snickers.

"You *told* on me?" She texted my fiancé about my behavior. "All right! I'll go." A tight ache is, in fact, radiating up and down through the muscles along my spine.

I really do need to work it out.

Dad watches me as I walk toward the guest room to change. I can't read his face. Is he enjoying his show? Is he worried about me? Himself?

Part of me wonders if he thinks he'll never see me again.

But I push that away like the ghost it is, and vow to live in the now, in my workout, at least for this moment.

❧

I KEEP MY PACE SOLID AS I RUN UP THE SMALL HILL ON THE DRIVE below Dad's house. The sun set about fifteen minutes ago and the Arizona night rolled in on the back of the crackle of cooling dirt and concrete, and the violet of desert shadows.

I could have asked Dad if he still has his punching bag and gone out to the garage and hit it until my forearms ached. That probably would have worked out the kinks in my neck better than running in the dark.

But my brain said *Don't bother me*. My gut said *Stay consistent*. I think the processing parts of my body wanted to not process for a while. My legs said *Move!* So I ran myself into consistency.

It's my way of meditating.

Breathe in the hot, dry air. Breathe out the oppressive heaviness of my bog-like thoughts. Drop my right foot. Drop my left. Inhale. Exhale. Swing my arms. Let my senses sense but set my mindfulness to the tension in my muscles.

My inner optimist wants my chin up and a smile on my face. It's tapping its toes and reeling off all the bullets it's positive we're about to dodge: New, fresh streams of income that will wash away all the bad. Doctors who will say, "Oh, it's nothing," and send Dad home right as rain.

But the dream resurfaces. The smothering, prehistoric palms. The unreal, too-intense greens and yellows. Hissing, iridescent insects shelled in what can only be my brain's interpretation of true red and true blue—the idealized visual frequencies against which all reds and all blues are compared.

Visually perfect and, in my dream, housing creatures both biting and poisonous.

I run into the shadow between two streetlights. Each light drops a solid cone of yellowish glare into what feels like the dusty, desert version of the darkness under the bed.

There be monsters out here, both real and imagined.

The street, the houses, the garden walls—they all glow violet-red from the sun's final, refracted rays. Here, the land takes hold of every beam of sunshine. During the day, it whips the light into the air as shimmering heat and buzzing insects. At dusk, the land clutches the sun to its bosom and refuses to let go, yet the day cools and deepens into blue-black as it slowly squirms away.

Sound travels better at night. I don't know why; I suspect it's an illusion more than a real phenomenon. Perhaps I hear better when I'm not squinting. Perhaps I pay better attention. Road noise stays constant until well after dark, but the animals and the plants stretch and sigh. Twigs break. Small creatures skitter. Yips echo between concrete and stucco, and claws dig into the hard-pack dirt.

A branch breaks. I glance over at the scrub between the road and a long, waist-high concrete garden wall.

Two amber eyes peer out at me through a particularly dense knot of branches and leaves.

My instincts kick in but I don't stop until I'm dead-center in the cone of a streetlight. "What do you want?" I say to the bush.

Another branch breaks. The eyes vanish into the shadows. My little friend stays hidden.

"Are you a coyote?" A bobcat would be less likely to get any ideas. A cougar would most likely walk right on by. A coyote, though, might decide to have some fun.

The bush moves. Something shuffles. But I still don't see my running companion.

"I really don't want to turn my back to you." Maybe I can scare it off. Slowly, still facing my amber-eyed friend, I inch away, toward the other side of the road.

A low, four-legged shadow backs out of the scrub against the garden wall behind it. And then it's gone, a furry and mostly silent dart of speed that vanishes along the concrete and around a corner.

I'm alone again. The streetlight over my head hums and clicks. Somewhere nearby, a car with a bad muffler rumbles.

Off in the distance, something howls, and I wonder if it's my amber-eyed friend.

Not far away, Isa's crossover waits in Dad's driveway. Very little light seeps out around the blackout curtains on the front of the house, but I can tell that someone moves around in the guest room.

I told Rob and Isa to take the bed, now that Dad's home. I even changed the sheets this morning. I'll pull out the sleeper-sofa and deal with the lumps.

The run, though, didn't loosen my back as much as I'd hoped. Plus I need to cool down.

Instead of going in, I walk around the garage and through the low iron gate. A layer of dust and sand covers the patio furniture. I swipe my finger through it as I walk by and sniff at it like some weird housing inspector or television detective.

I don't know what clues I think I'll find among the dirt and desert. Maybe a little bit of desiccated insect. Nothing unusual here, just normal signs of neglect in a normal widower's home.

A halo of bluish light filters around the corner of the house. Someone's in Dad's studio.

Maybe Rob's checking up on Dad's work. Maybe Isa came out to offer another artist's eye. Maybe it's the coyote—or a thief.

But the shuffling and the groans sound specifically human—and slow and methodical as if whoever is moving around in the shed cares enough not to break anything.

"Dad?" He should be sleeping. The doctors said he needed to take it easy, no stress or exercise or working. Plus, we have a long drive ahead of us tomorrow.

Only one of the studio doors hangs open. Inside, the LED lighting bounces off the white ceiling and throws an even brightness into the corners.

Dad sits on a stool in front of his stack of ghost-infested canvases. His hands drape between his thighs, but he doesn't slump. He doesn't move at all.

"Dad?" I say again. Is he okay?

He looks over his shoulder. The diffuse but bright light hides the hollows and shadows of his face. Dad looks almost healthy again.

Almost. So much of the muscle his broad frame should carry has vanished, and for some reason, it's more obvious in here. The contrast with the father I grew up with—the big mountain of a man who did such delicate work—is too much for my brain to handle. The dissonance sits in the pit of my gut. It twists and twirls and makes it difficult for me to look away.

"Camille called while you were out. Dan is down with the fever. It'll be a week before they're safe to travel." He shrugs. "Sounds like Bart's still healthy."

"He's been vigilant with the hand sanitizer." I'm not surprised Dan's sick. "Camille was sniffling something terrible before I flew down."

"Rob talked to Sal already." Dad returns his gaze to the paintings. "They're leaving tomorrow anyway." He shrugs again. "Duty calls."

"He'll stay if you ask him to." Isa's brother Mack would probably take Rob's class for a few days, if needed.

"It's okay. They both have work." Dad points at the stack. "I don't think this is what the Arts Council wanted when they commissioned a 'Salute to Snowbirds.'"

They wanted something celebrating the widening of the local culture, not darkness.

I wipe my face on my t-shirt. "Does Rob know you're out here?"

Dad frowns. "I'm not a child."

No, he's not. "You're sick."

Dad doesn't move. "I have work to do."

He always had work, as did Mom. They worked hard but they were there for us when we needed them. Most of the time, though, they let us take care of ourselves.

"Because you have a good head on your shoulders," my mom used to say. "We trust you and your siblings." Then she'd wag a finger. "But if you need help, or need questions answered, or a ride, or anything else, you ask, got it? Be proactive."

Excellent advice for dealing with the world. "What's going on, Dad?" Evasiveness isn't going to get him cured.

He stares at the canvases. "I don't think I can handle the drive tomorrow." No part of him moves. No slumps or twitches.

"The appointments are set." We have everything under control.

"Tom..." Dad grasps my wrist. "You understand, don't you?" He nods toward the canvases. "They need to be finished. I can't do anything else until *they're* done."

He's using work as an excuse? "Dad!" I yell. I shouldn't, but I know what's happening here. I *do* understand.

His life isn't in order. He's afraid of leaving unfinished business and chaos and deep sudden wounds inflicted on the people he loves.

"You can finish them when we get back from Phoenix. You need that biopsy. You need to get checked by—"

"Tom!" He looks up at me and I can't tell what's more hollow—his eyes or his words. "I'll go. I promise." He rubs his face. "But I'm tired. I need a day or two before facing yet another trial."

He points at the canvases. "*They* need finishing."

When my father gets like this, there's no arguing with him. It's as if he's possessed. I've seen it before. Dan calls it Dad's "witching moments." He used to do his best work while like this.

But it often interfered with the rest of life.

"You won't go, will you?"

Slowly, Dad shakes his head *no*.

"When they're done?"

He nods his head *yes*.

"Please don't be like this." I almost add *This isn't what Mom would want*, but hold my tongue. He doesn't need that guilt. *I* don't need that guilt.

"Don't be like what, Thomas?" He's staring at the canvases again.

But this *is* my father. The eerie confidence in his proclamation that Rob and Isa's baby is a girl. The tornado of psychic energy—some brilliant and bright, some dark and frightening—rising from his person. The ripping down to the studs of the emotions of those closest to him.

And I wonder if I'm the same way.

I pull another stool next to Dad's. "There are new therapies for the depression."

A grim smile cracks his hollow face. "Ah, yes, my mood disorder." A pained laugh erupts from his throat. "I *need* to work it *out*."

Dad points at the canvases again.

It's been over a decade. Twelve years, to be exact. This "need" should have dissolved a long time ago.

But sometimes wounds don't heal correctly. Sometimes they fester.

That knot in my stomach jumps and spins yet again.

Mom always told us that she trusted us to do right and to ask what we needed to ask. "You think it's malignant, don't you?"

Dad inhales deeply. He bows out his chest and he sits straight. "Would I have lost this much weight between your gallery show and now if it was just some little growth?"

"Maybe," I say. I don't know. I'm not a doctor.

I nod once and only once because I feel numb except for the spinning and the jumping in the pit of my soul. "But you promise me you will reschedule. Please."

My dad's nod mirrors my own. "I promise."

A promise. A moment of cooperation. A capitulation.

Outside, the coyote howls.

CHAPTER 24

Samantha

A small family could live comfortably in my Imperial Sands room. I have access to a large wall safe, two coffee makers, a microwave, and a refrigerator. The huge tub could handle at least three people.

The scent of rosemary wafts off the thick towels and lavender off the sheets. Even the curtains smell nice. I was greeted by a tray of assorted chocolates and coffees placed lovingly in the center of my cushy mattress.

The bed itself, with its mounded dunes of pristine white sheets and overly plump pillows, is the size of a small nation. The flat screen bolted to the dresser looms over the roomscape. Three mirrors accent the generically "classy" spiral-patterned wallpaper; two of them are subtly positioned in such a way as to allow a good view of any bed activities.

Which, right now, involve a spread-out arc of gallery space photos, shots of Juri's other, mysterious property, and a lengthy marketing proposal open on my laptop.

It's all to tempt me with an Assistant Supervising Manager position, one that would report directly to him. One that he says he ultimately plans on expanding into an Assistant Vice President role, if the first wave of his hotel and resort proposals go well.

I'm to be in charge of overseeing the zeitgeist of a new generation's entertainment options—to shepherd Olson Companies into new, wide-open terrain. No boredom. No consultant-produced word salads. Travel, yes, but I would still be based at home, in the Olson Companies main campus.

My dream job.

Or I step back and rep my fiancé into building a mountain inside the fun, new, Olson-made world.

The proposed gallery space is actually spaces, inside at least three separate, distinct and holistic areas; they are exactly where I expected them to be, extending through the concourse connecting the old half of the Imperial Sands with the new. But what's most interesting is that they feel accessible not just to art lovers, but to people looking to love art.

The mysterious property is just as magical. It's embedded in the natural beauty of the Southwest and, I think, if handled well, could provide an active vacation destination. Juri plans to whisk me away for an in-person tour tomorrow.

And Juri believes I'm the talent he needs to mold this venture into something.

He didn't say much about salary other than to promise "at least double what you're making now." *Double*. I need to research market rates, but at least double would bring us up above what Tom and I were making combined before he got laid off, and I think I can negotiate more. We'll be set. Tom won't have to worry about replacing a job he didn't want anyway.

But the opportunity to get his work into the wonderful gallery space would evaporate.

My gut's been twisting and spinning. I haven't yet called Tom. He and Isa know about the spaces, but I haven't told him about the job offer.

I run my finger over a glossy photo of what's to become the gallery space, then over the thin, vellum-like leaf of the proposed architectural plans. "Thomas Quidell" could be the name on the plaque next to the door. The following gallery could have "Isolde Wellington Quidell." The world could open up to the beauty made by two very talented artists.

I don't know what to do.

My phone rests screen-down on the mattress inches from my thigh. Should I call Tom now? Wait until tomorrow, after I have details?

The phone rings. I snatch it up.

"Hey, love," Tom says. He sounds exhausted.

My tummy does the jumping thing again. I feel as if I'm about to bounce right off the bed. "Is everything okay?"

"He refuses to go to the clinic in Phoenix."

I push off the mattress. "Why?" *Does he want to die?* I think.

Tom sighs heavily. "He won't go until he finishes a couple of pieces."

"I don't understand." Mr. Quidell's health trumps any piece, not only for him, but for his sons, too.

"Strangely, I think I do." Tom sounds as if he's rubbing his face. "Listen, I thought I'd let you know. Rob and Isa are leaving in the morning." He pauses. "Dan won't be flying in tomorrow."

He must have caught Camille's fever.

"I wish he wasn't sick. Maybe my brother can talk some sense into Dad."

Maybe, I think.

Should I tell Tom about Juri's job proposal? Add to his already numbing level of stress?

Probably not.

"Do you want me to drive down?" My plan was three days in Vegas. "If I leave now, I'll be there a little after midnight." It's not that far.

Tom's silent for longer than I like. "God, I want to see you."

My gut's twirling flips into joy.

"But I think he needs fewer people around, not more."

And then right back into crunched-up fear.

I hear a door open and close. "I need to help him get the work done. He promised he'll go if he finishes the work." His voice cracks. "Sammie...."

"Are you sure you don't want me to drive down?" I could call Juri. Tell him it's an emergency.

"Isa was excited about your messages earlier." Tom sounds the opposite of excited.

"I'm working on it." I'll do everything I can for them.

"Thank you." He pauses too long again. Another sigh flows through our connection. "Please be careful out there, okay?"

Of course I'll be careful, I think. "Don't worry about me," I say. He has enough on his mind.

"I love you," he says.

"I love you, too." I need to help him. I need to get this deal set up so that it brings joy back to my fiancé's life.

Because I think he's about to lose his father, too.

CHAPTER 25

Thomas

Morning glare bounces off the windshield of Isa's crossover. The air smells fresh, and it's not too hot yet, which makes loading the car easier.

Isa layers sleeping bags and a couple of old shirts over her camera and lighting cases before closing the back of the car. "There," she says, and wipes her hands on her jeans.

Rob offers a quick hug. "You're going to be okay here?" he asks again. He's been asking the same question all morning.

"We'll be fine." I nod toward the house. "Dan's fever has to break sooner or later."

Rob's lips bunch up. "I can't miss class." He's been repeating that sentence all morning, too.

"I know." I pat his arm. "Dad will work. I'll set the new appointments. It'll be fine." But I think Rob knows I don't believe my own words, either.

"We're ready." Isa takes Rob's hand and pulls him toward the front door. He glances at their car before motioning to me to follow them back into the house.

Isa's already to the couch by the time Rob and I close the front door. Dad sits against the arm, his blanket over his legs and lap, and a sketch pad in his hands. Charcoal smudges his face and hands.

At least he's working.

Isa squeezes Dad's hand and kisses his cheek. "You'll make the appointment the moment the pieces are finished, right?" She points at his current sketch.

"That's the plan," Dad says.

Isa touches her belly. "Please. Jerry wants you healthy at her first birthday."

Dad inhales and sets down his pad. For a long moment, he stares at Isa's belly, then reaches out to touch her cheek, but stops with his hand halfway between his pad and his daughter-in-law.

"You take care of the little lady." His hand moves toward her belly as if pulled by a ghost, but he stops that movement too, and pulls back his fingers.

Isa squeezes his hand. "I will, Jeremiah."

Dad grins.

"I want progress reports." Isa points at the sketch.

Dad chuckles. "You and the doctors."

Isa glances up at Rob, who frowns.

And once again, I think Rob knows Dad doesn't believe his own words.

Rob walks over and sits in the chair next to Dad's spot on the couch. "I'm flying out of LAX in three days," he says. He's been repeating the plans all morning, too.

"You need to work, son." Dad taps his sketch. "We all need to work."

Rob drops his hands down between his knees as if he's trying to make sure Dad doesn't see them twitch. "Dan will come once he's no longer contagious."

"I know." Dad squeezes Rob's arm. "This is my choice."

Isa pats his shoulder. Rob looks away.

Dad glances at me, because, I think, I'm the one who is supposed to understand.

He needs to excise his ghosts before he allows anyone to excise whatever he has growing under his lungs. If he doesn't, they'll just leak into his chest cavity and fill up the space left behind by the biopsy.

I don't think Rob would understand if I tried to explain it to him. He doesn't understand the physical effects of the dreams. He doesn't feel the lumps and the pits and the certainty that the images and concepts—the textures and colors and motions—inhabiting Dad's brain actually do pulse across his skin. That they do, in a literal way, wrap around his heart.

I've read about synesthesia—about how for some people, numbers have a color, or a tone, or a texture. How, in their heads, the intangible literally becomes tangible. How they are touched by ghosts—and how they see the souls of things that should not have a soul.

Now I wonder if Dad has always had a bit of synesthesia. If he's always been driven to paint because he feels the process sweep across his skin, smells the art, and not just the paint. If that's why he never let it go, never stepped back enough that his need to paint didn't send Mom into overdrive right along with him.

If that's why he needs to finish his pieces. They're an open wound right now, and he can't go into an operating room if he's already bleeding out.

Part of me wonders if I inherited some of Dad's perception. If that's why I haven't finished my giant painting of dream jungles. Maybe I can't stand the thought of the pain that will come with healing *my* wound.

Dad looks like he just read my mind. One eyebrow twitches upward, along with the corner of his mouth. But then he looks away, and the look switches over to "concerned parent." He pats Isa's hand again. "I'll send you an update twice a day."

She glances at Rob again. They both hug Dad once more, then stand and walk toward the door.

Rob leans close. "Call if you need me to come back."

I pat his shoulder. "Go take care of your family." I look back at Dad. "I have this."

And this time, I try to be confident enough that Rob believes what *I* say.

CHAPTER 26

Thomas

S ometimes, Dad works flat. He'll lay a canvas on the floor, or on his table. Flat gives you a different perspective on the work; an angle that's not really *real*. No one will look at the piece as if they're about to crawl onto it, or walk over its colors and patterns.

Yet sometimes the piece feels as if you're on your knees. That it's me—or Dad—who's about to get sucked into a constricted tunnel and popped out on the other side of the looking glass.

I throw open the studio doors and open the transom windows. Dad wants the evening heat, so we paint in the wide open air. Sweet, dusty air breezes in. Hot and dry feels oppressive and itchy to me, but it makes Dad happy, so I flap my t-shirt and persevere.

Traffic noise from the street rolls around the house and into the backyard, as does the laughter of a neighbor. A dog barks. The sizzle— and the savory, mouth-watering aroma—of grilling meats follow.

Dad doesn't seem to notice. He sits in his lawn chair and leans over his laid-flat, ghost-infested canvas—the one with the bloody woman. Slowly, he runs his fingers over the bruise-colored smudge of the phantom woman I'm sure is my mother.

Another neighbor laughs. I hear the clinking of beers.

My stomach growls. "You hungry, Dad?" Maybe I can get him to eat.

I glance at his painting again. Maybe I can get him to go inside for dinner.

The ghost on the canvas does exactly what it's supposed to do—it makes me uncomfortable. I twitch if I get too close to the piece. My fingers jitter and my neck tenses up. I don't want to look at it even though I fully understand what it is that I am looking at.

Do I have it in me to make something like that? To put onto a canvas something so bloody and raw?

Dad waves his hand in my general direction. "Go get a sandwich." He drops the hand back onto the canvas and slowly, carefully runs the very tips of his fingers over the paint as if he's reading braille.

"You need to eat." I touch his shoulder and his shirt bunches up under my fingers like the striations of the paint stroke under his fingertips.

Like his fucking ghost.

He's dying. The thought fully manifests in my mind's eye as if it's some goddamned movie scene complete with swelling sound design and optimal, Academy-Award-level cinematography. As if it's a photo Isa took.

Or a painting that's so far beyond my talent level I'm angry at my own brain for making this thing to tease me—which is why I know the content of the thought is true. If it were false, would my subconscious put so much effort into making me see it?

Probably not.

Dad looks up at my face. He blinks once and his eyes narrow. "I'll eat when I'm done for the night." He taps the canvas. "It won't be long."

I can pull off not eating and sleeping because I'm healthy. Dad, not so much. "You need to take care of yourself," I say.

Dad only grumbles something indecipherable.

"We'll get the work done." I promised him that. "But you need balance here, Dad. You won't have the strength for the trip to the Phoenix clinic if you push yourself more than necessary."

Dad sits back into the weave of the lawn chair. It squeaks and rattles, its frame groaning about my father's still-big bulk, and slides a little away from the canvas.

He grips the arm rests. "I know, son." His fingers whiten, but he looks at his hand and lifts his palm away from the chair. "Your mother used to tell me the same thing all the time."

I must look confused because he shakes his head.

"Not about doctor trips." He stares at the painting. "About balance. About caring for you and your brothers. About paying attention to our marriage. About small things like not inflicting my mess on the rest of the family while still being able to work."

He points at the second lawn chair and I dutifully pull it over.

Dad taps his heart. "What's in here is no more or no less important than what's out here." He sweeps his hand in the general direction of the world. "Sometimes one will pull harder than the other. Sometimes one will push you away. But it's all about balancing the two."

He sweeps his hand at the painting. "That's what she used to tell me. Yin vs. yang. Personal vs. professional. Soul vs. duty."

Dad closes his eyes. "I still don't understand."

Do I? I don't know. And for some reason, the dream of jungles—the organic, prehistoric plants that wanted to eat my soul and the concrete, man-made concourses that wanted to engulf my body —comes back.

I pat his arm. "I'm not sure it's a dichotomy." I'm not sure it's trichotomy, or a quad-chotomy, if there are such things. I think it's just the world.

And the world will find a way to eat your soul by taking your livelihood. Or by taking your life.

Dad touches his ghost painting again. "This is what I see when your mother walks into a room." Dad runs his finger over the blood and burning of the edge. "When she died, it turned black."

I sit back in the chair. Is he still seeing Mom?

Dad shakes himself as if he's just realized what he said. "Her memory, now. Her memory still walks with me." He taps his head. "Of course I no longer have her here to shake off the ash." He touches the painting again. "Or the blood."

I touch the painting, too. My fingers reach out before I realize I've moved my hand and my skin touches the object that's been making me squirm since I opened the studio for Dad. The thing that makes me want to back away.

The image is not what I remember of my mother. I had just reached her height before she died. I hadn't gotten used to it; every time she walked into a room, I expected someone taller. Someone with a grander presence.

I still do. I expect every woman to take up the same amount of space in my life that my mother did for me as a child.

And, I think, as she did for my father.

Sammie fills that space. Sammie moves and the currents she causes light up the air around her. She is the space and the space is her, and all I do is paint the full context of joy she brings me.

She is no different from an expanse of a white, sandy beach, or the fullness of the heavens in the sky above Sedona.

Dad pulls back his fingers. "This isn't right." He flicks his thumb against his pointer finger as if pushing off dirt. "This isn't what I want to see."

Right there, right in front of me, I see his posture change. He's declaring the ghost image as a single step in his journey to his finished work.

I recognize the blinking and his small head movements. I see it in the set of his lips. When I was a kid, I saw him do the exact same movements before he took a work off his easel and set it gently to the side—as if it were a signpost he needed to heed, not a painting.

This piece, the one with the bloody, black ghost, is just that. It's a sign pointing him in the direction he needs to go, and it needs to stay the way it is. It needs to be not-finished, to be only half an image. Because it's not what my father wants the world to see even though it is part of what needs to be shown.

I wonder if it is, quite literally, what is wrapped around my father's heart.

"Okay, okay," I say as I pull the canvas off the table. I'm up, rummaging around in his clean canvases looking for the correct one. The correct size. The correct shape. The right base.

"How's this?" I hold out a fresh canvas, one that's closer to square, and also bigger than the black, forever-unfinished piece.

Dad's eyes widen for a moment, then he nods toward the easel. Slowly and with great care, he flips through his sketches. His finger traces something I can't see, but I'm pretty sure I know what he's found: light. White light. Clean, brilliant light. How do you paint something so formless?

My father knows how. For him, that light has texture and wave. It has a surface and it sings.

"Help me set up." He waves at his paints.

I step toward his supplies—but stop when my phone rings.

"Sammie," I say into my phone. Dad stops fiddling with his easel and looks over.

"I set up a deal," she says. Her voice sounds hollow and I don't know if it's because of the connection or if it's coming from Sammie herself.

"Are you happy with it?" Rob reminded me to trust Sammie to do her job. She can handle both the predators and the fluffy bunnies. I have no excuse for acting... possessive. Because that's what I was doing —acting possessive.

Damn it, I can't be that way with my fiancé.

She pauses. "Yes."

Something's off. "What's wrong?"

Another pause. "Nothing. It's a good deal. I just wish you were here and able to celebrate. That's all."

But I wonder. "Are you sure?"

Sammie chuckles. "No predators here to worry about, Mr. Quidell." I hear her shuffle something. "Juri's setting up a whole new entertainment arm of the Olson Companies and wants to fill a lot of positions."

He offered her a job, I think. I know it in my gut. And all of a sudden my sense of predators rears up like a horse frightened by a wolf.

"How's your dad doing?" She's changing the subject.

"Better," I lie. What did Juri Olson offer? More pay? Excitement? "What are the Olson Companies looking to do?" What if he's about to suck her away?

Across the studio, Dad slumps into his chair.

She pauses too long again. "It's grand and complicated. You saw the gallery spaces. They're superb."

Dad returns to fiddling with his canvas, but I can tell he's paying more attention to my conversation than he is to his work.

"I wish I could come down and visit." Sammie can only take so many vacation days, and she's used most of them for this trip. Someone has to hold the insurance-paying job, after all. "Maybe I'll fly in next weekend?"

"I think Dad would like that."

A soft grin appears on his face.

"I can't wait to meet him in person. I'm sorry it has to be because he's not feeling well." She sounds wistful. "Juri wants to talk contracts over dinner and I need to call Isa yet." More rustling. "I'll call you later? Make sure you eat, okay?"

And not just cereal, dances through my head. I chuckle. "I will."

"I love you," Sammie says.

"I love you, too." I do. I wish I could shake the sense of predators waiting to rip us both apart.

"You won't have to worry about the mortgage anymore, with this deal," she says. The wistfulness is gone and the "something's off" has returned to her voice.

"I'll call you later." And her voice is gone, vanished into the eternal night once again.

I stare at the phone in my hand. Dad fiddles. We don't say anything for a long while.

Dad sits back in his chair. "Speak, son," he says.

I tuck the phone into my pocket. "I think Juri Olson is trying to steal Sammie."

Dad laughs. "*Steal* her?"

I roll my eyes.

"What, exactly, is he trying to steal here, Thomas?" My father sounds very father-like—and looks it, too, even frail and sitting in a lawn chair.

"I don't know." Part of me wants to scream that he's stealing my woman, but that's both stupid and simplistic.

And, as Dad implied before, utterly unbalanced.

This isn't all about me.

Dad runs his finger over his nice, new, clean canvas. "What's your gut telling you?"

I stare at the transom window behind Dad. The sunset blazes across the distant mountains as flares of red and orange. The same mountains which stand physically between Sammie and me right now.

And I still don't know, but I sense predators.

Dad glances at his ghost-infested painting, the one he set aside. "Go to Vegas."

I can't, I think. I can't leave him here alone.

Dad points at my nose. "Don't be like me. Don't ignore your gut and don't ignore your muse." He twirls his finger. "Go."

"But..."

"I'm fine! I'll work." He slaps the arm of the chair. "I'll call Sal. You need to go."

Sammie needs me.

The gut twisting happens again. The same acknowledgement of the art in front of me that happened with the Kandinsky in the Art Institute. But this time it happens when I think about Sammie.

I run for the house to gather my bag for the drive to Las Vegas.

CHAPTER 27

Samantha

Neon flashes outside my room's window. On the street below, drunken tourists live it up. Several blocks away, magical fountains spray magically-lit water to beautiful, well-loved music. People gamble. Some shop for souvenirs. Others find the strip clubs and visit old school Vegas.

And others just try to get their jobs done before their shifts end.

Juri flew me to his mysterious site earlier today in his white-and-red Olson Companies helicopter. I pushed up my sunglasses, straightened my pencil skirt, and played attentive copilot.

He clicked toggles and pressed buttons. I grilled him on details of his new site and tried not to think about the intimacy of the moment. This wasn't the first time he'd flown me to a remote location.

Juri kept it professional. We flew over the site. He pointed out the roads and the trails. I gazed in awe at the sheer beauty of the red hills and the scrub—and I think I now understand Juri's drive to build. He wants to tame the site, but not too much. He's asking me to help him with the wrangling.

But which path toward that wrangling do I take? The one good for my soul, or the one good for Tom's?

I pull the comfy, plush Imperial Sands robe close to my skin and adjust the towel wrapped around my hair. The second thing I did after Remy dropped me off at the hotel was to take a long bath to wash away the Nevada grit.

The first thing I did was spread the contracts Juri handed me at dinner across the big, fluffy bed.

I won't sign anything until I have a lawyer check them, though they're both pretty straightforward. One, I take the Assistant Supervising Manager position. I'll answer directly to Juri. If my evaluations go well, I'll be on track for a Special Projects directorship in a couple of years, then on to a vice president position.

The other contract covers first-look rights to existing works "to be specified" and an extensive list of commissions, as well as a guarantee of gallery space for both Tom and Isa. It's basically a signing agreement for my artists.

One contract or the other, Juri said. He can't take me on as part of the Olson Companies if the Foundation guarantees Tom the commissions.

Just the one contract for my artists, I told Tom.

Carefully, I gather the contract for me. I tap the pages and straighten them into a sleek, smooth set before slipping the paperclip onto the corner. The second set I tap into its own bundle and clip together. Then I lay first one, then the other, on the huge desk in the corner of the room.

More lights flash outside. A siren blares. An emergency vehicle races by on the street.

I could get dressed. Take a walk down to the gallery space connecting the Imperial Sands East to the new Imperial Sands West. It's not technically open, but it is a foot-traffic concourse, and I could take a few photos in the evening light for Tom and Isa.

Or I could close the curtains. I need to sleep. I have a long flight tomorrow.

But I just stand here in the spike of neon glare coming though my window. It's a high-energy world out there. A playground of debauchery and wishful thinking in a city that's alive because everyone needs a little not-my-normal-life time.

How is that different from selling GMO yogurt? Juri's offering me a chance to transform the playground into something a bit more authentic.

The hotel phone rings. I screech and jump as the damned ring reverberates through the room and sets my teeth on edge.

I swipe up the receiver.

"Ms. Singleton? This is the front desk."

"Yes..." Why is the front desk calling me? Juri's people would call my phone.

"Ms. Singleton, a..." I hear mumbles. "...Mr. Thomas Quidell is here to see you."

"Tom?" Tom drove up from Sedona? "Is everything okay?"

I hear rustling. The desk clerk hands over the phone. "Hey, beautiful," Tom says.

My stomach knots up. "Why are you here? Why didn't you call? Is everything okay?"

"I wanted to see you." He sounds both bemused and disappointed. "Do you want to come down and get me? Should I come up?"

I look at the receiver in my hand. "Why didn't you call my phone?"

Tom laughs. "I forgot to charge mine before I left." I hear the clerk mumble something. She laughs, also. "What's your room number again?"

I give him the info. I hear instructions about hallways and turns, and Tom follows up with an "I'll be there in a second."

I set the receiver onto the phone's cradle. Tom drove up from Sedona? He didn't sound upset. Maybe his dad changed his mind and decided to cooperate with the doctors. I swipe my phone off the bed. Did Dan fly in even though he's sick? Camille didn't text me anything, though. What if—

A knock on my door echoes through the room.

I toss the phone onto the bed and throw open the door.

Tom immediately moves across the threshold. He moves so fast I don't have time to get a good look at his face or to read his expression.

He engulfs me with his big arms and chest, and I am suddenly, completely, caught in his embrace.

He presses his face against my hair. "Are you okay?" he asks.

Why would he ask that? "I'm fine." I try to push him away enough that we can talk, but he holds me tighter.

"Please," he whispers.

Did something bad happen with his dad? I snuggle against his warm chest and wrap my arms around his waist. "Are *you* okay?"

He steps into a shadow and I still cannot see his face clearly. It doesn't help that he turns away to close the door.

"I had a bad feeling after you called." Tom splays his hand over the door and his fingers press into the wood as if it's clay.

I don't know what to say. I don't understand his "bad feelings." I've always considered them part of his sensitivity to his environment, sort of like people who can pick out camouflaged animals in the woods, or pilots who can see through fog.

But the thing is, he hasn't been *here*. He's been with his dad. So I don't see how his bad feelings could possibly apply to Las Vegas.

Unless the bad feeling is jealousy, or the same set of insecurities that made him stomp around the loft ranting about "predators."

"I have this under control, Tom." I realize after the words come out of my mouth that I sound a little too much like my mother. I respond by frowning at myself.

Which probably makes me look just like my mom.

Tom watches me over his shoulder. His hand comes off the door and he stands his full six-two height. He squares his shoulders. His back and his neck tense.

Thomas Quidell stands in front of me the big, formidable male he is.

God, I love his body. I love *him*, all of him, but every once in a while his constant awareness of his intimidating physical presence vanishes. His focus moves and all of a sudden, he's a protective man-mountain who has no time for some asshole's shit.

I've seen him turn it on other men—he did with my ex, Rick. And right now, I get the distinct sense that it's aimed at a man who is not in the room.

Which pisses me off at the same level of heat as my boiling desire to climb up his torso and into his arms.

Thomas Quidell causes me a painful level of oscillating emotional whiplash.

"Tom!" I throw my arms into the air and walk toward the bed. "Will you *please* let me do my job?"

When I look back, his gaze is firmly on my ass. It travels upward to my breasts as I turn toward him, and stops again. When he looks up at my face, a very quick flash of lust moves across his cheeks and eyes at the same time a pout hits his lips.

I'm not the only one experiencing dichotomous emotions.

I don't know what to say. I don't know what to do, either. We could cover over this moment with sex. Hot, intense fucking that would last hours mostly because we don't want to talk.

It'd be one hell of a short-term gain, but long-term? Not so much.

I've been here before with guys. Covering dysfunction with fucking. I used to do it all the time. My libido is a harsh mistress and pleasing her was always easier than fixing my shitty relationships.

It happened with Juri. It happened with every single man I've ever been with, except the man in front of me right now. Only Tom cared about the long-term.

But if he's going to be over-protective and over-sensitive and over-... I don't know what to call it. He's *Tom* and he is who he is, but I am who I am, too. I *like* doing my job.

I rub my neck as I watch the pout vanish into a stance I can only describe as "I'm angry because I'm afraid." This particular dichotomy —anger on one end, fear on the other—screams off him in waves of clenching fists and barely-controlled tension that makes me feel as if he's about to storm out the door and hunt Juri.

Which won't help anyone.

Maybe I can coax some concrete understanding out of Tom— something beyond "I had a bad feeling" and "They're all predators!"

"*Why* do you have a bad feeling?" I walk toward him again. "Give me something I can follow up on." I wave my hand at the window. "If you're sensing something here that I'm not, I'd feel a lot better if I knew what it was."

Tom frowns. "He's a *predator*, Sammie."

Yes, yes, I almost say. *Juri is a wolf.* Though I think one of those cuddly vampires might fit better, and as with all vampires, he has rules he must obey.

If he fucks with me, I'll stake him in the heart.

I'm beginning to think Tom's definition of "predator" is not the same as mine. That somehow we're looking at two different pictures of the same thing, and the thousand words spoken by mine are a completely different essay than the thousand spoken by his.

"I got a contract, Tom. A good one, for you and Isa." I guess I've already made my choice. I guess it's Tom. "I don't want you to lose this opportunity."

Not him, not Isa, not Dan or Jeremiah, either. Not because Tom couldn't get a handle on his feelings.

Not when I'm willing to give up a dream job for myself because giving up the long-term with Tom is unacceptable.

Not when I've worked this hard to make this deal.

"I don't want it." Tom rubs the top of his head. "Not if I have to give up my integrity."

I want to slap his arm, right at his shoulder. I want to haul off and smack him *right there.* Maybe knock him out of his selfish, self-centered space.

"Just your integrity?" How is it that my Tom, the man so sensitive to the world that he can paint its underlying truth, cannot see the obvious in front of him?

He frowns again. "Yours, either."

"What?" Does he think I sold myself to Juri? "I worked a deal, Tom! That's all!"

Working deals is what I do. It makes me happy. Happier than working communications around yogurts and cereals. This deal to bring art into Juri's entertainment world felt right. I felt like I did something worthwhile.

And Tom thinks I pimped out myself to do it?

"Go back to Sedona!" I yell. "Go be with your family!" I look around for my jeans and a t-shirt. "I need to go for a walk."

Tom steps closer. "Why?"

I drop the robe on the bed and stand naked in front of Tom. Naked, but for the first time since meeting him, I don't feel like touching.

My fiancé stuffs his hands into his pockets. "Dad told me to come here. He said that I need to pay attention to what my gut tells me and it's been telling me since I got laid off that we're vulnerable. That..."

He looks up at the ceiling and closes his eyes as if he doesn't want to see my breasts anymore.

I pull on my jeans and t-shirt. No underwear, no bra, no socks, either, just enough fabric that I won't get into trouble walking the hallways. I swipe my key off the dresser top and stomp toward the door.

"Sammie!" He follows me like a damned puppy. "I don't know what to say. I don't know what to *do*."

"*You* feel vulnerable, Tom. *You're* the one all twisted up here, not me." It's true. "I've been trying to help and you're pissing on it because you can't tell the difference between your bad dreams and what's in front of your nose."

I open the door. I want to yell more. I want him to see reason, but I know he won't.

Reason isn't something he sees. He needs to touch it, to rub it between his fingers and get it under his nails. He needs to sketch it and fill it in with determined strokes of blues and greens.

Tom needs to shape and create reason.

I love him for it. I love how I don't understand his process, and learning his ways—watching him work and seeing his art manifest—is intoxicating. I love how we complement each other.

But right now, he's valuing his way of seeing the world more than mine.

A lot more.

I let the door close behind me when I turn into the hotel hallway.

CHAPTER 28

Thomas

I follow Sammie into the hallway. The Imperial Sands is a standard Vegas hotel full of standard Vegas artificial glitz—fake, white-washed crown moldings over vinyl wallpaper printed with some lush-looking Victorian pattern all in a wide, grand-feeling hallway. The lobby was just as artificial and imaginary.

I don't want to be part of this. I don't want Sammie to be part of it, either. I don't want it to gnaw at our souls until it opens a vein and we both bleed out.

"Sammie!"

She just keeps walking.

"Honey!" I jog up and walk beside her. "This place is *fake*. It'll eat us up and spit us out as little plastic trinkets."

Nothing I make for Juri Olson's company will have value other than as marketing.

Sammie pokes at the elevator button. "You are as pigheaded as your brothers." She crosses her arms over her chest.

"What the hell does that mean?" I'm the level-headed one. At least that's what Sammie usually tells me.

"It means, Thomas Quidell..." The elevator doors open and she steps in. "... that you're thinking only about yourself right now."

I step in, too. She doesn't stop me. But she continues to hold her arms over her chest as if she's embarrassed that she ran out of the room without a bra.

Her luscious breasts are distracting. Round, soft-yet-firm, and with only the knit fabric of her t-shirt between them and my hands. Her nipples poke out too, and I want to rub my face between them.

I also want to bang my head against the elevator wall. It's as if my brain wants to push her away while my body wants her as close as I can get her.

The rush of adrenaline isn't helping to suppress my horniness, either. I almost ask if she wants to go back to the room, work out the physical, and then talk about it.

But I think that will make things worse, not better.

The elevator is a shiny chrome box with extra glass and loud pings as we drop toward the hotel's lower levels. "Where are we going?"

My stomach jumps upward because of the downward velocity.

Sammie straightens and turns fully toward me. "You're going to see what you're giving up."

Why can't she *see* what's happening here? Yes, I feel vulnerable. But at least I realize my vulnerability. She doesn't.

The door slides open. We're on the lobby level, but this elevator bank opens into what looks like a long shopping-mall-like concourse. Laughter filters in. Pop music fills the air. There's a cart selling t-shirts not far away.

We're about to step into a human-filled, concrete-jungle gully.

I must have shuddered, because Sammie puts her hand on my elbow. "Come on," she says, and pulls me into what looks like one of the connector passages between hotels that allow the tourists to move from one casino to another without going into the heat.

People mill about, but mostly they walk between the potted palms and the occasional benches. To our right, laughter and music roll from an open restaurant and bar. Big, flat-screen signs dot the walls next to doors, all advertising the spa services and other pampering. But mostly it looks like a non-place to walk through while traveling to a real place. It's soul-sucking, but not in the way my dream felt.

Sammie pulls me to the right. We walk by another, smaller bar, and around poster after poster advertising shows. Showgirls spin on one; a magician works magic on another.

The crowd thins out.

We turn a corner and the concourse widens, though most of it is closed off and behind temporary walls, except for a wide glass door.

I peer into the dark space. It gleams, pristine and lovely, and about twenty feet from the door, an empty pedestal sits under a skylight with some type of electronic veiling system.

Sammie points at the space. "Juri wants to turn this into a place of beauty and joy for the people who stay in the hotels." She taps the glass. "He wants to install a park full of art *right here*."

"This is one of the gallery spaces?" Across the way, behind another wall of glass, another wide open space waits.

"One of them, yes." Sammie lets go of my arm. "There's another at a ranch he just purchased." She sighs. "He's trying, Tom. There's a demand for authenticity and he wants to supply it to the masses. He's smart enough to know he needs creators to do it. Marketing alone won't provide the experiences he wants to deliver."

It still feels fake to me. Fake and dangerous.

"This is what I've been fighting to get for you and your family. This opportunity to make something real in a place that needs some reality. *I* worked for this. *I* fought back those predators you keep warning me about. Will you at least acknowledge that I'm good at what *I* do? Please?"

She's so angry with me she's shaking. I think she wants to slap me across the face because I'm pigheaded.

Is this what Dad warned me about? Not to ignore my muse?

But what about my gut?

I lift her up into my arms. I don't know what else to do, or how else to respond. She works as hard as I do—harder, I think, because she multitasks better. She knows what I need and she's trying to help me find it.

Because she loves me. She's loved me since the moment we met and I've been a dumbass trying to force her to change instead of trusting her.

I can't lose her. I can't lose the feel of her skin against mine, or her lips on my temple, or the soft sounds of her breath. I can't let go of the sweet scent that is *Sammie*. The wonder and joy in my soul because she wants me. But she can't get hurt, either.

I set her down and gently kiss her lips. "Did he offer you a job?"

For a second, she looks confused. "I'm not taking it. The gallery space is better. For you and Isa. It's—"

"What would you be doing, if you took the job?" I don't want her to take it. I don't want her playing with wolves every single day, but I'm beginning to wonder if that's what my Sammie *should* be doing. She's a wolf tamer.

"Setting all this up for the Olson Companies." That's all she says. No mention of salary, or travel, or any of that. Just the core of the work.

I splay my hand over the glass wall. The desert evening flows over the lone pedestal inside and I can't help but wonder if I'm about to lose her. Is she going to be ripped away from me the same way Dad is about to vanish?

"I feel like I can't breathe," I say. I feel surrounded, unprotected, vulnerable. Battered and alone with jaguars and wolves inside a smothering jungle.

Sammie curls her arms around my neck and I drop my head to her shoulder.

"I think my dad wants to die," I whisper. This is the first time I've vocalized it. There's been an edge of denial to all my thoughts about his refusal to go to Phoenix. *He's going to die* carries a thread that he might still be willing to fight it. *He'll go after he finishes the work* pulls it taut.

"We don't have to deal with this now." She kisses my cheek. "Okay? Come back to the room."

"I don't know what to do." Sammie is here and she's alive. Nothing is going to jump out from behind one of the huge potted palms and steal her from me.

I need to keep telling myself that. Maybe I'll start to believe it.

She's frustrated. I can tell—she's still shaking. But Sammie isn't going to let her frustrations stop her from helping me.

She touches my cheek. "Let's go upstairs."

CHAPTER 29

Samantha

Our room door thuds against the jamb. A slice of hallway light bursts around its edges, a backward bracket of white filling the space between Tom and me and the bed.

He glances at the neon reds and blues pulsing in through the open curtains, then squints at the brightness flooding in around the door. Another couple moves down the hallway and by the door, both laughing in the low, growling way two people about to fuck laugh, and I can't help but wonder. Are they drunk? Are they happy? Will they look at each other in the morning and ask "Hey, what's your name?"

Tom spreads his fingers over the door. His head moves as he listens to the people pass by, but he looks down at his feet. Then he pushes the door closed.

Neither of us turns on the lights. The flow of the city is enough; it's often enough at home, too. Tom would occasionally look out the window, an ironic, lopsided grin on his face, his fingers moving along an imagined fedora, drawling some noir line about "bathing in the light of a typhoon, baby."

He glances over his shoulder at the reds and blues flickering over the bed, his shoulders both tense and slumped, and his body language unimpressed.

I don't think he has it in him to play hardboiled tonight.

I touch his cheek. "Hey," I say, and run my hand down his neck, to the rock-like muscle of his shoulder.

Most of the men I've known carried their stress as knots in their lower backs. Tom does as well, but it also cinches up his deltoids. I think it's because he uses his shoulders to position his hand and brush while he creates.

Slowly, I maneuver myself into the tight space between his body and the door. He doesn't step back or alter his footing; he just stares down at me with piercing-yet-distant eyes.

I press my cheek against his chest and wrap my arms around his waist. I was right about his lower back—the muscles on either side of his spine feel rock-hard and immobile under my palms. His heart beats a little too fast against my cheek. And his breathing feels distant.

I wish I knew how to help him. I wish I *understood*. But Tom perceives the world differently than I do, and from the physical responses of his body, I wonder if his demons are more real to him than mine are to me.

How can he listen to reason if he's all locked up and in defense mode? He needs to calm down before we can talk.

And sex suddenly flickers over from a way to distance us from our problems to our way of coming together. It's no longer fucking.

It's the intimacy we both need.

I press my breasts against his chest and my forehead into the crook of his neck. My hands roam up to his shoulder blades, and I curl one leg around his, but I don't kiss. I don't wiggle or grab his ass.

"Sammie," he groans into my hair. His arms scoop under my backside. He lifts me off the floor and my back slides up the hard finish of the door.

The pocket of my jeans catches on the handle.

We pitch toward the side, both yelping, both laughing, but Tom has me. He has us both, and he sidesteps and pulls us clear all in one strong, graceful movement.

For a second, for one brief, shining moment, his beautiful blue-green eyes light up. He smiles one of his brilliant, bold smiles.

Laughter bubbles up from my core.

"I wish I could paint the way you do." I stroke his face. "So I could show you how much I love you."

He chuckles and grins again, but his eyes soften. "If I'd have said that, it would have sounded corny. From you, it makes me glad to be alive."

"We complement each other." I kiss his shoulder. "You paint. I run the business."

He tosses me a little, to get a better hold on my backside. "You're getting heavy." He tosses me again and glances over his shoulder at the bed.

I drop my feet to the floor. Tom steps back, but I take his hand and when I duck under his arm, I pull him around so he's facing into the room instead of toward the door.

The light in his eyes vanishes. He blinks once, slowly, and stares at the open window. "Jaws and gnaws," he mumbles.

Stop it! flares inside my head. All the frustration, all the anger that made me drag his sorry ass down to the gallery space erupts up from its smoldering embers.

I'm running out of patience with my man and I just want to pluck out his chest hairs one at a time. Just pinch and pull and watch him wince. Maybe he'd pay attention to what's real and not his phantoms.

I push him forward. He goes with my shove, but rotates as he moves, so his back is to the bed. The smile vanishes into a frown. He looks as if he wants to ask me what I'm doing but I don't give him a moment. I pull my t-shirt over my head.

That got his attention. I wrap the shirt around my wrist and rub it over my chest and belly the way I'd use a cloth to wash my skin.

His eyebrow arches.

I point at his chest. "Take off your shirt."

The eyebrow arches higher. He doesn't move.

"Now." If giving him orders gets his attention and gets him out of this funk, even for a moment, then orders will be given.

Slowly, he pulls his t-shirt out of his jeans. He continues to exaggerate his eyebrow arching, but cooperates.

The t-shirt drops to the floor. My Tom stands between me and the bed, his broad shoulders backlit by the city's glow, and flexes his biceps.

He knows what that does to me. A smirk appears, and he flexes again, but this time he holds out his wonderful, masculine hands as if to cup my breasts.

Tingles start in my belly. They flow out into my body along their familiar, well-traveled paths—first up into my breasts, then out along my shoulders. They fire up my neck and I swear my vision sharpens. Other tingles move into my groin, and then down my thighs, to my knees.

"Take off your jeans." He's not going to get to me. I'm going to make this happen, but on my terms.

Tom turns his hips away just enough to bring his belt buckle into the light thrown by the window. He tightens his core and flicks the end of his belt out just as a flash of blue washes over his abs.

I lick my lips. Maybe I growl too, because Tom looks a little too pleased with himself.

I grab the end of his belt and tug it from the buckle. His hands fall away and he watches my fingers work, his eyes hooded as if he can't quite get his spooks to back off. The demons gnaw and he can't quite send them packing, not even for sex in a Vegas hotel room.

The frustration growls from my throat, thick and annoyed and animalistic. I yank his belt from its loops and push him toward the bed again.

He steps back, but doesn't drop onto the mattress. He holds himself rigid with his concrete-like back muscles and gives me yet another eyebrow arch.

"Jeans." I point at his fly. He's going to undo them himself. He's going to lift out his legs one at a time.

He undoes the button, but stops as if waiting for me to finish the job for him.

I smack his left ass cheek with the belt.

Tom's eyes widen. His mouth rounds but he catches his surprise and the bratty eyebrow returns.

I smack his other ass cheek.

The jeans drop to the carpet.

The head of his cock springs free when I curl in a finger and yank on the waistband of his super-soft, low-cut, black boxer-briefs. Tom groans; I know that when he's hard, he hates the pressure of his clothes. Hates how they constrain and rub and distract him from everything but how uncomfortable his erection is.

Now is when I usually circle my tongue around his tip. When I take him into my mouth and lick him once, twice, three times—all to wash away the discomfort. I bend forward and press my ass up to give him a tease and make him forget about the pressures of the world.

Not tonight.

I let go and his waistband snaps against his cock. "These too."

Tom groans again. "I thought you liked my underwear."

I can't tell if he's serious, a smartass, or as frustrated as me. Maybe he's all three.

I snap his waistband again.

Something in the way he stands changes. The distraction vanishes into a new tension that feels equal across all of his body. It moves upward from where I snapped him with his waistband, outward from his chest, and up into his shoulders. I feel it slide down his bicep and into his forearm.

His expression changes. He has no idea what I'm about to do and his eyes focus on not only my body, but his own, as well. Muscles flex and relax, but stay ready for whatever I might throw at him.

He is suddenly, completely *here*—and my gorgeous Tom is at a loss for what to do.

The boxer-briefs drop on top of his jeans.

Tom looks down at his cock. It bounces slightly with his heartbeat, its head sweeping up-down, up-down as if moving on a clock between two-ten and two-twelve.

He pushes his hips forward as if daring me to wrap my fingers around his shaft, drop to my knees, and take him deep into my throat.

I grip his belt instead, holding it in front of my bellybutton and tightly between my fists.

"Now my jeans." I don't move.

A wicked grin appears on Tom's face. He's enjoying this. I've broken the spell and opened up a whole new avenue to vent his frustrations. It's new. It's different. It's dangerously fight, flight, or fuck.

Slowly, deliberately, Tom wraps one hand around his shaft. The other, he slips under his balls. And just as slowly and deliberately, he adjusts himself, lifting and tugging, stopping only to swipe his thumb over his tip.

I respond by slapping his belt against my palm. The leather pops against itself, and a crack echoes through the room.

"*Hmmm....*" Tom unbuttons my jeans. He tugs on the zipper the way he tugged on his cock, but he doesn't pull it down. Instead, he tucks a finger between the fabric and my skin, his palm flush against my belly.

His touch is electric, his hand warm and dry. He presses the tips of his other fingers into my flesh in a star pattern between my bellybutton and my pussy, but slides the finger in my jeans up and down in a way that somehow tickles.

He's *tickling* me. The pressure from his other fingers almost hurts. I wiggle my hips to force his finger lower and with one fast, intense movement, Tom rips open the zipper. His hand scoops between my legs.

He cups my pussy and *squeezes*.

I gasp. Tom chuckles.

"Finish the job." I slap his belt against my palm again.

Tom drops to his knees as he grips the waistband of my jeans. He yanks the fabric down my thighs and past my knees, but stops once it hits my calves.

His eyes narrow and he grunts as he takes in the puddle of denim around my legs.

Tom rolls my waistband over, then over again, tightening my jeans into a thick, constraining knot around my legs. "Done," he says.

His lips dance gently over my lower belly, but his hands work up my legs in gripping, kneading pulses.

"You are a tease, Mr. Quidell."

The wicked grin returns.

I rub the edge of his belt along his hairline, around his ear, across his jawline, and tap it against his lips. "Lick me."

A flash of annoyance flickers through his eyes. His lips tighten.

Tom yanks my hips toward his mouth. I twist uncontrollably inside my denim bonds, my balance upset by the pull, and almost fall over, but Tom's fingers dig into my flesh.

He grinds his face into my pussy.

An arch of electricity pulses through my core. I lean precariously backward, but Tom's arms tighten around my middle as his tongue probes into my folds.

I drop the belt. The buckle clanks as it hits the carpet and Tom jerks a little as if the sound startled him. Or maybe he was waiting for it.

His tongue hits me like he's running a long race and damn it, he's going to win.

"Tom…" I whisper as I dig my fingers into his hair. This is the Tom I want—the Tom I *need*. The man who gives even when the world is chasing him around in circles.

Part of me wants to push him down onto the bed and lick him in tight, smooth swirls, up his shaft, across his balls, over his tip the way that always gets him off. But my instincts tell me he needs something new, something that offers another route. One he's never seen before, even as he gets his escape through sex.

"I dropped the belt," I say. "I—"

Tom lifts me off the floor.

Straight up, his arms around my thighs and his face still in my pussy. He stands up from kneeling while holding onto me and the whoosh, the speed, and the teetering all combine into a rush so strong I release a long, stuttered moan.

I'm floating in the air a good three feet higher than I should be. I grip his shoulders, trying desperately not to cinch my core too much but still hold myself upright, and just let my body soak up his strength.

All the power, all the energy, all the high-tensile humming of his working muscles. All his frustrations and fears and his needs.

He groans into my pussy and the vibration moves from his tongue to my clit.

I try to hold my orgasm. I do. But I've never been good at edging and controlling myself, especially with Tom.

My back arches. Our center of gravity shifts. And the next thing I know, I'm dropping fast toward the mattress.

I hit hard. The entire bed bounces upward with me. The frame groans and the headboard whines. I slide on the sheets but Tom is over me, his hands on my waist as he steadies both of us.

He rips off my jeans. Then he's on top of me again, his hard cock rubbing against my clit. A new wave of orgasm slams into my belly and everything—my chest, my arms and my legs—flutter. A loud, guttural moan rips from my throat.

Tom seals his mouth over mine. I taste myself on his tongue, but mostly I taste Tom's salty warmth.

His own guttural moan mixes with mine when he thrusts in. He's not gentle, but he's not rough, either—he's strong. Powerful. In this moment with me, he's in control.

We sway and rock, and the bed bangs against the wall. *Thud*, he slams into me. *Thud*, I kiss his chest. *Thud*, a new, loud groan rumbles through the room.

Thud.

Tom pushes up on his hands as he increases his speed. His chest reddens and his head tilts back.

His cock jerks just as he drops his full weight on top of me.

"Don't mean to squish you," he mumbles. But I don't think his muscles are working well enough to move off me. For the first time since he lost his job, his back feels loose.

I curl my arms around his head and gently kiss his cheeks and eyebrow. "*Hmmm...* I'm glad you came for a visit."

"That was new." He rolls off, but he pushes up on his elbow and rubs small circles across my upper arm and shoulder.

He sounds as if he wants forgiveness for being rough—as if he believes he did something wrong.

I roll onto my side and cuddle in close to his wonderful, warm body. I stroke his calf with the side of my foot. I stroke his shoulder with my fingers. And slowly, gently, I stroke his neck and chin with my lips. "New isn't always bad."

Tom flops us both onto the bed, me on my back and him with his arm draped over my belly. He presses his face into my neck as he caresses my hip.

"No," he whispers. "No, it's not."

"Are you going to be okay now?" I don't want to shatter his calm. I want him to find a moment of comfort.

Tom curls around me. He tucks a leg between mine and drapes an arm over my hip. He settles his head against my shoulder.

But mostly, his breathing slows. He syncs to me.

The rhythm feels right. It feels alive and conscious and... together.

"When's your flight home?" he asks.

"Tomorrow afternoon." Time for me to go back to the GMO word salad.

"Come down to Sedona next weekend. Please. I want to introduce you to Dad." Tom's arm tightens.

I stroke his hair. "When you go back, talk to him about your gut feelings, okay?" Juri Olson isn't the only predator circling Tom.

Tom only nods. I feel some of his stress flow back into his body.

"Sleep," I say. "I'll lay out the contracts tomorrow morning. We can talk about them." I kiss his temple. "We can talk about everything when the sun's up."

Tom nods again and that little flux of tension releases. "I don't know what I'd do without you."

I cuddle closer. The truth is, I don't know what I'd do without *him*. I think tomorrow we need to talk about what that means.

CHAPTER 30

Thomas

I know I'm in a swanky hotel room in Las Vegas. I know Sammie, wrapped in smooth, white sheets, sleeps next to me. Blinding sunshine and heat leak in around the blackout curtains. Yet I'm swimming in thick air and unseen things slither around the roots of the bed and through the drawers of the dresser.

My eyes pop open and the swank comes suddenly and completely into view. The golden wallpaper shimmers in the shadows. Other, unseen guests knock walls and plod across floors.

I rub my eyes, taking care with my elbow to keep from waking Sammie. She sighs and rolls over onto her other side, and the blanket mounds up around her lovely, smooth hip, yet I can't shake the feeling of things slithering. Of ghosts and predators hiding in the shadows.

When did I become so fucking paranoid? Why won't it go away? And here I'd hoped that Sammie slapped that shit out of me last night.

The need to pee chases me off the bed. I pad naked across the room, rubbing at my belly and trying to ignore my morning wood, still seeing thick, heavy shimmering out of the corner of my eye.

The plush terrycloth robe Sammie wore when I appeared at the door sits as a pile of ghostly white in the shadows next to the bathroom and I can't help but push my toes into it as I walk by.

The terrycloth feels softer than I remember from last night. I lift up the robe and hold it in front of me, and the fabric cascades over my arms and chest. The weave is so thick it's almost velveteen.

I press it to my face, hoping, I think, to catch Sammie's scent, but I sense only the lack of smell that comes with unscented industrial detergent.

It's confusing. I pull the robe away from my face. Too much confusion. Too much fear. How am I supposed to see the truth of the world if I'm like this?

Someone moves in the hallway in front of the door. Light shifts in front of the peephole and the little dot moves between bright and dark, bright and dark as if the person is pacing in front of the door. A muffled male voice makes it across the threshold and sounds as if the man is talking into his phone. I hear short, clipped words, pauses, and a definite "later."

He knocks on the door.

I glance at Sammie. She moans and rolls over again, but doesn't wake up.

I glance back at the door. I know who it is. I sense him through the thick, fireproof wood. He's outside my fiancé's hotel room in his four-grand suit with his five-grand CEO data-driven phone in his hand because he wants to take her to breakfast. Show her a little fun before she flies home. Make the deal all that little bit more tantalizing.

I pull the robe around my shoulders. It's small on me but that might not be a bad thing.

The chain rattles as I pull it off the lock. The door handle catches and knocks as I push it down.

Juri Olson stands facing down the hall, toward the elevators, his phone in one hand and his other hand in his pocket. He's in full rich-guy swagger—until he looks up from his small screen and realizes I'm not Sammie.

"You must be Thomas Quidell," he says, and extends his hand to shake.

I have a good five or six inches on Juri Olson, and probably forty pounds. He, though, has more money than God.

"Yes. You must be Juri Olson. Sammie's told me about you." With my height, I have the dominant handshake position. I don't let Juri Olson forget it, either.

He scowls, but at least he doesn't attempt to look around me and into the room. "Sam's flight goes out at two-thirty. I stopped by to see if she wanted to discuss any last details over breakfast."

Why does he know the specifics of my fiancé's flight? I scowl right back at him.

"Will you be joining us?"

I swear his eyes narrow and his lip curls, and the sense of *predator* screams back into my consciousness.

Do I go with "We have plans"? Or a simple "Yes"? Do I leave this to Sammie? I should, but part of me screams that if I do, I'm leaving *her* vulnerable to an attack.

Juri Olson needs to understand that she's with someone worthy of her.

"Sammie showed me the gallery space last night." I roll my shoulders. "I approve of your designers, Mr. Olson." This time, I add an ironic sniff. "The interior looks promising but I wish to see it in person."

Juri Olson snorts and shakes his head. "Put on your clothes, Mr. Quidell. I'll take you down."

CHAPTER 31

Thomas

The elevator descends. We're treated to a clanging, annoying rendition of some random eighties soft-rock song. Juri Olson stands on the other side of the big car, once again facing perpendicular to me. He stares at his phone. His other hand sits on his hip in an "I'm about to pull my gun" or "Look at my badge here on my belt" position. All he needs is a pair of Oakley sunglasses and he'd look as if he just walked off that Vegas cop show about crime scene investigators.

"Sam will be joining us?" He continues to stare at his phone for a moment, then tucks it into his rich-man's suit jacket and turns his body square to me. The hand doesn't come off the hip.

"When she's ready." Sammie shooed me away before bounding into the bathroom to make herself "presentable."

She is the most presentable woman on the planet, but when dealing with Juri Olson, a certain level of professionalism is expected, even though the man had the gall to show up at her hotel room door.

I don't care if he was "in the area" or not.

"So, Thomas—may I call you Thomas?" Juri nods toward me but

aligns himself with the elevator door.

"Tom is fine."

Juri Olson nods once. "Tom..." He sounds as if not saying the "as" at the end hurts his throat. "... Sam's judgement and taste are impeccable."

He holds his face flat as if to insinuate that he will be the judge of what's impeccable and what's not.

"It is," I say. I hook my thumb into my pocket.

The elevator stops and a sweet, recorded voice says "Lobby." Juri waves me forward.

To my surprise, he doesn't have any problems matching my pace. "Has she explained to you what we are looking for? The basics of the commission?"

I nod. "You're looking for destination art. Works that speak to the adventurous soul of a generation that values experiences over possessions." Now I sound like a damned brochure.

Juri Olson seems to approve. He points up the long concourse toward the gallery spaces. "People come to Las Vegas for the spectacle." He waves his hands in the general direction of the Strip. "It's time for a new kind of spectacle. One that attracts the new aesthetic."

"And here I thought you wanted pretty pictures of naked ladies."

Juri Olson laughs. He swipes a card and the glass door to the space pops open. "That, my young friend, is completely up to you." He motions me through the door.

The air inside the gallery space is... different. I can't immediately put my finger on it, but it feels fresher. Cleaner, but not in a "cleansed" sort of way. Clean, as if blown through a thousand miles of rain forest.

I walk toward the pedestal under the skylight. The glass refracts. It sparkles, but with specificity.

"We're inside a timepiece." Or the beginnings of the creation of a timepiece. Not a clock, but something more. This gallery space off the horde-filled spectacle-space connecting one Vegas hotel to another could be so much *more*.

A place of movement and a place to make solid the passage of experience.

Juri Olson watches me flat-faced but with piercing eyes. "I offered

Sam a position. One that will allow her to shepherd the creation of whatever this place is to become, Thomas."

He walks toward me. His hands are on his hips again, in the cop pose. For some reason, I doubt he does that with Sammie. Part of me wonders if he is unconsciously trying to make himself look bigger.

Does *he* feel threatened? Does Juri Olson see *me* as a predator?

"She told me." I don't want her working for this man.

I need to fully admit to myself exactly what it is I'm feeling here—anger that he swooped in. Jealousy. Fear. It's all swirling in my head.

I'm not sure I want to work for him either, but the space calls to me. A sense of time, of ceremony wants to manifest here.

I could let it flow from my fingers. It could be me.

Or Sammie could shepherd another artist. Someone who isn't me.

The intensity of *choice* mixes with what's flowing from the *other* spout—anger at my dad for refusing to do what I want him to do. Jealousy that he experiences the world differently than me. Fear that he's going to die.

It makes the air thick. It fills that rain forest with attacking fronds.

I close my eyes for a beat, and breathe. These images, they are a part of me. They're a part of how I see the world. They give me a layer of reality that is solely mine. My father has his own layer. Sammie, hers.

Everyone wants a piece of everyone else's reality. My dad's ghosts want a piece he refuses to share with the doctors. I have pieces I want to share, and others that make me feel hunted when people like Juri Olson come sniffing around.

Sammie decided to give up a part of hers to help me explore a part of mine. Not to protect me. Not to make us the most money or get me the most prestige. She wants me to move beyond what nips at my heels and *create*.

"I will only work for her." The sentence pops out of my mouth and I swear I'm not the one saying it. It feels as unreal as my nasty dreams.

And I just let it talk.

I spread out my arms. "This space needs ceremony. I know what to do." Probably. Like many of my projects, it's beginning to take form. The whole "timepiece" thing is in the air. I sense it, feel it, breathe it.

"It's one or the other."

Juri Olson's words pull me from my creative space. My body doesn't like it. I snarl.

His eyes narrow again.

"Bullshit." He's fucking with Sammie. He's fucking with *us*. "You'll get the best deal if we come as a team."

The door clicks. I step to the side.

Sammie stands behind Juri Olson in her jeans and one of her nice casual tops, her hair in a ponytail. She looks casual, but professional.

The expression on her face says she heard what I said.

Sammie walks by Juri Olson, nodding once, and right to me. She places her hand on my chest in a "calming the beast" sort of way—her touch is light and just to the left of my heart—but she's looking directly at Olson.

"Yes," she says. Her hand lifts off my chest. "The energy inside is... exquisite." She steps toward the pedestal. "The contracts are not mutually exclusive if the Foundation hires me as part of the commission award, Juri." She runs her hand over the pedestal much in the same way she touched me. "I could move to Olson Companies in a few years." She waves her hand at the gallery space. "Or I could take over the Foundation for you."

The smile she throws him is as wicked and wolf-like as anything he could possibility make.

I chuckle.

"Who better to wrangle your brilliant talent than a brilliant wrangler?" Sammie says.

Juri Olson's mouth opens, then snaps shut. He shakes his head before pointing at Sammie. "You, my dear, are way too good for that cereal company you work for now." He shakes his head again.

"I know." Sammie moves back toward me.

Juri Olson pulls out his phone. "I want you both on board before the end of the month, got it?" He taps at the screen. "The longer this space sits empty, the more money I lose."

Olson puts the phone to his ear and with a dismissive sweep of his hand, walks away toward the crowds strolling his concourse.

CHAPTER 32

Samantha

I found watching Tom and Juri circling each other like two alpha wolves more exhilarating than I probably should have.

When I looked through the glass door into the gallery space and saw Tom in the same shoulders-forward, piercing-eyed, tight posture he used when I was living with the asshole ex-boyfriend who called me a little bitch and a skank, I knew Tom and Juri were duking it out on some level.

A level that involved me.

They aren't assholes. Well, Tom's not an asshole, but he has been teetering between flight and fight, and I think the two states have set up a painful, shrieking resonance in his head. It makes him crabby. And uncertain. And not my Tom.

But I also think last night's push-pull sex helped.

When I walked into the gallery space, I felt Tom's wonderful baritone filling the space more than heard it. I felt the intent behind his "Bullshit" more than understood the word.

He sounded as if he'd commanded a wild animal to stand down. He wasn't afraid of being stalked anymore.

Stalked by expectations, his own and those of others. Stalked by loss. Stalked by the fear that he can't make it out of the hole he's been thrown into.

Poor Juri got the brunt of it.

I run my fingers over Tom's chest again. His body has returned to its normal humming state, but he feels different than he did last night. He feels correct now.

"We make a good team, don't we?" Tom says.

I love the trust this man gives me. I love his smile and his core strength. And I love that I was able to help him find his way again.

He tips his head and looks up at the skylight. "The hotels on either side must throw shadows during the day."

Tom's still-humming body tenses as he concentrates. There's art here and he's going to uncover it.

His composition snarl surfaces.

I have no resistance to the snarl. I didn't when we met, and I have even less now.

I slowly place my other hand on the other side of his chest, and just as slowly, I run both down his front. When I reach the top of his hips just above the waistband of his jeans, I rest my hands but make little circles with my inward pointing thumbs.

Tom's attention drops from the skylight above his head to my teasing fingers on his torso. "*Hmmm...*" he says, and glances at the glass door leading out of the gallery space and into the concourse foot-traffic area.

He snakes his hand farthest from the door—the one no one would be able to see—up my hip and under my top.

He's careful. My top isn't moving much. From the concourse, we'd look as if we're hugging.

His big palm covers my breast and the electricity of his touch makes every hair on my body—at my nape, across my arms, over my scalp—stand up. I moan softly and the next thing I know his mouth descends onto mine. His lips work over my top lip, my bottom, then down my chin toward my neck.

He's not looking at me. He's watching the door.

I groan and push him off. I want his full attention. "You are too damned distracted." I stick out my tongue.

The way he stands turns cocky. He smirks. "What are you going to do about it?"

He opens his mouth just enough I glimpse his tongue.

It's a fight to keep my hands off his belt buckle, and even more of a fight to keep from pulling out his shirt and rubbing my face against his abs.

Tom glances around the gallery space. It's just as empty as it was when we came in, just as bright, and mostly viewable from the concourse.

Mostly. Tom's hungry gaze returns to me. "Over there." He points over his shoulder.

The temporary wall blocking most of the gallery space from the outside world jogs into a corner not far from the door, and makes a small alcove that faces the podium and the skylight. A broom, a mop, a bucket, and a "Caution: Wet Floor" sign sit in it now, their handles against drywall, all lonely and forlorn but brightly lit, like everything on this side of the wall.

We should go back to the room. "What if Juri comes back?" What if a security guard comes through? What if some elderly tourists figure out what we're doing?

Tom stares at my breasts. His wonderful fingers and wrists do small movements, little indications of the scenarios running through his mind right now—a thumb across my lips. A finger in my pussy rubbing against my clit. His hands on my head as I vacuum his cock.

It's all there. It's as if he's painting the space between us with exactly the movements he wants and his actions override all thoughts of getting caught.

My Tom is most definitely no longer stalked.

I swear I have a small orgasm. A little one, like a pre-tremor. The earth's about to move and this is one of those little waves out front that most people can't sense.

Tom smirks again. God, he's as good at reading me as I am at reading him.

We really do make a good team.

I look over my shoulder at the door. No one out in the concourse at the moment. I look back at Tom. He loosens his belt and undoes the button on his jeans.

"Does it hurt?" I point at his fly. "The pressure on your erection from your zipper?"

Tom shrugs. "It's... noticeable."

He can't be in pain. Not from sharp metal teeth. I push him toward the alcove.

"Careful." Tom kicks the bucket to the side and it grates across the bare floor. The mop, he tosses onto the floor next to the bucket. The broom, though, he ignores.

Grit swirls up in the alcove. It's not as pristine in here and slight hints of grease and singed wood waft up with the dust. I wonder if the workers use it to store tools when they're in here, or if this corner is used for cutting and sawing.

Tom bumps the corner of the alcove where it meets the outside wall. The entire assembly wobbles. Outside, in the concourse, muffled voices say "What was that?" and "The wall moved."

"Oops," I whisper.

Tom holds his finger to his lips.

I nod. He wants the thrill of semi-public sex, and I am not going to allow this moment to pass.

Tom squeezes both my breasts, first the left, then the right. He pinches, but my top and my bra keep him out, so he yanks up the fabric of my shirt and down the cup of my bra before sweeping his thumbs inside my cups.

"I want you to take your nipple clamps to work from now on," Tom whisper-growls. "I want you to put them on before you leave and I want you to endure the bumpy bus ride home constantly reminded of me."

He pinches my nipple.

Laughter pushes through the wall. Someone walks by.

I slap my hand over my mouth.

Tom pulls out his hands. He grabs the "Wet Floor" sign and drops it flat on the floor in front of him, then waits for me to comply.

I kneel down on the plastic. It's not a lot better than the concrete floor, but it's enough to protect my knees.

I finish undoing his belt and releasing his fly. Tom presses his hips forward just enough to rub his still boxer-brief-covered cock against my face. The soft cotton brushes my cheek, my lips, the tip of my nose. The cock underneath is rock hard and, I suspect, dark with his engorgement.

I ease the waistband of his boxer-briefs over the head of his cock. Heat hits my face, along with Tom's clean scent.

I close my mouth and purse my lips to kiss his cock, but he touches the top of my head. He wants me to hold still.

Tom grips himself and curls his abs and moves just enough to bring the head of his cock against my pursed lips. He rubs a bead of pre-cum against my mouth and when I begin to open my lips, he pulls back.

His hands descend into my bra again, and this time, he pulls both my breasts out and together.

He taps each nipple with his cock, rubbing and slapping.

I can barely handle it. He knows I like oral—giving and receiving—and he's always good about giving me what I want. Having his cock so close but held back is almost enough to make me scream.

I open my mouth to moan but he drops my breasts and gently lays his hand over my lips. He nods at the wall.

I nod too, to indicate I understand.

Tom glides his fingers over my mouth, then slowly pushes it closed again, the way it was before he rubbed my nipples. His eyes narrow and his face sets in approval.

He pushes his thumb against my lips, but I don't let it in. I want only the velvety tip of his cock.

A new, stronger look of approval works across his face. Tom curls his fingers into my hair. He doesn't tug me closer. Instead, he presses toward me and spreads another bead of pre-cum over my already glistening mouth.

He presses harder. I part my lips just enough to let me flick the tip of my tongue over his slit.

Tom groans deep in his chest. He keeps his mouth shut and the sound rumbles out along his bones to his fingertips, and to my scalp.

He pushes into my mouth but pulls back before he hits my throat.

I grab his hips. I know what he wants—a deep thrust, followed by a couple shallow ones. He wants the rhythm. He wants my tongue adding a cool harmony to the sensation of suction on his cock. He never specifically asks. He never demands, either. He never takes.

But I know what he wants.

I pop my mouth off his cock and look up over his abs at his face. Confusion surfaces and his eyes narrow. Did I hear something? He tilts his head, listening. Did he thrust too deeply and set off my gag reflex?

I lick his cock, base to tip.

I want him to yank down my jeans and fuck me on the floor, against the wobbly wall, on the pedestal in full view of the concourse—I don't care. I want him banging against my clit as he stares into my eyes with all the intensity his ocean-colored irises hold.

But I also want this new, no-longer-stalked Tom and his new, dominant attitude.

Tom grins. His hands weave into my hair again and he rubs the underside of his cock against my lips. Then he's in my mouth again, hot and velvety against my tongue. He slides in, but not too deep, then out, but not so much that he breaks the vacuum I made.

A deep thrust. I take it and more, and another moan rumbles outward from his bones. I lick and pop my lips over the ridge at the base of his head, but I keep him in my mouth.

He watches me through half-closed eyes with a slack mouth. Red creeps up his neck and onto his cheeks. His speed increases. His fingers spasm against my scalp.

"Oh..." Tom's abs tighten—but he pulls out.

He moves behind me, his back against the wobbly wall and his hands forcing my jeans down my hips. I drop forward, my hands landing on the dusty concrete floor, as Tom maneuvers me enough to get access.

He slides one finger through my folds, and when the tip hits my clit, he slides in a second. He works them both across my nub, rubbing first one way through my wetness, then the other. Fire erupts through my entire body.

KRIS AUSTEN RADCLIFFE

His fingers vanish from my body. I almost yell *What the hell* but he slams his cock into my pussy.

I shudder as the orgasm blasts through each and every one of my muscles, but somehow manage to keep quiet. It washes through me like waves against my sun-warmed skin. My sense of direction shifts. I re-orient toward what's coming at me—Tom. His strength. His attention.

Tom slams into me one last time. His cock jerks. He leans over me but stays in control. No knocks against the wall. No sounds. Just one of his perfect grins.

Someone on the concourse side taps the wall. Someone else laughs.

I hold my finger to my lips. Tom pulls out and adjusts his underwear and jeans. We're up and presentable, the mop and bucket replaced and the sign set against the wall, before the next person walks by.

Tom pulls me into his arms. "Meeting you was the best thing that has ever happened to me on every level of my life."

No one has ever said anything like that to me. Not in normal, public moments. Not in private, post-sex moments. Not over dinner or while watching a movie. Not when finding a quarter on the ground and not after making a big business deal.

I tuck my head against his neck and hold onto to him with all my strength.

Tom runs the pad of his thumb over my engagement ring. "I want to design bands." He kisses my temple again but looks over at the skylight. "We should be prudent, right? Wait until the contracts are signed." He hugs me again. "Thank you, by the way, for being the best there is at your job."

No man other than Tom has seen all my worth. "I *am* good, aren't I?"

I wouldn't be at this point without him. He helped me see beyond the wall I'd put up around myself.

I run my hand over his hip. "You're the one who sold him on the art."

"I'm good, too." He sucks on my earlobe. "I love you, Samantha Singleton."

"Yes, you do." I'm never letting him go. Never. "I want to marry you today." I do. Rob and Isa married in Nevada, so why not us?

Tom pulls me tight against his body. "Don't you need to fly home in a few hours?"

I pull out my phone and pull up my boss's number. "Hold on," I say, as my phone rings. "Tony. Hi, it's Samantha."

"Everything okay?" He sounds genuinely concerned.

"I'm not going to make my flight home this afternoon."

"Oh?" I hear him rustling. "You need more time?"

"Tom and I are going to get married today." I glance up at Tom. "Then we're going to spend a few days with his dad."

Tony's silent for a moment. "Do what you need to do, Sam."

"Thank you, Tony." He's a good guy. "I'll have news when I get back."

I hear a soft chuckle. "Other than getting married?" He pauses and I suspect he leaned forward and now he has his elbows are on his desk. "You're quitting, aren't you? I've been wondering when you'd move on."

"Tony, we can't talk about this over the phone. You know that."

He chuckles again. "When will you be back?"

"I need to reschedule my flight. I'll text you when I have everything set. I promise it won't be too long." I may be moving on, but I still have a job to do.

"All right." Tony really is a good guy. "Bye, Samantha Singleton."

I tuck my phone back into my pocket as Tom curls his arms around me again. "Thank you," he says, as he leans his cheek against my temple.

I breathe him in—all of him. His intensity and his strength. His pain and his joy. "I love you, Thomas Quidell."

Tom grips my waist and lifts me into the air. "So, Elvis or aliens?"

I extend my arms like a showgirl. Tom has me. I won't fall. "Whatever are you talking about?"

"If we're going to marry in Vegas, we need to make it a memory."

Because it's all about the experience. "Elvis, baby. It's always Elvis."

CHAPTER 33

Samantha

The wide sliding-glass doors of the Imperial Sands part and hot Vegas air slaps my eyes and nose. It's dusty today, and the sun beats down with that desert "buzz" that always accompanies heat mirages—except here, it's road noise and not insects.

The doors of the Imperial Sands open into a corridor of sorts—a wide-open, covered area framed by tall plants. It offers a view of the road, but the plants do block an immediate view of the hotel's entire parking and waiting area.

While Tom was in the shower, I made a phone call. Remy is here somewhere. Tom, though, thinks we are going to his car, which is parked in the hotel's garage.

I tug Tom into the heat. "Time's a-tickin', Mr. Quidell."

My stomach growls, but we don't have time to pick up breakfast. The chapel had only one opening this morning if we wanted Elvis to perform the ceremony, so we hot-footed it through showers and dressing.

Tom had been almost giddy when he saw that I'd packed my indigo pencil skirt. He walks next to me in his "best" jeans and a white button-front shirt, his leather cord around his neck, fresh-faced and with his sandy hair still slightly damp.

For the first time in a long while, he looks happy.

"Though we may need to stop for a Danish," I say.

"No passing out at the ceremony, unless you want Elvis to catch you, baby." Tom does a quick finger snap and Elvis-like hand wave before snatching me by the waist and dipping me like an expert ballroom dancer.

"Tom!" But I love it. I love how he takes in the world around him and brings out what needs bringing. Right now, he wants me as happy as he feels.

He swings me back to standing. "My lady." He bows and throws a flourish toward the parking circle behind the big plants.

I kiss his cheek and walk forward for a better view.

Just around a bushy, dark-green, tree-like plant, Remy leans against his limo. He smooths his black chauffeur suit jacket and tips his black chauffeur hat, a huge smile on his face, and sweeps his arm toward the limo.

Tom looks at the limo, then at me, then back at the car. "You hired a limo?"

Except he's not acting as surprised as he should be. He smirks as if he knows exactly what's going on.

"Not quite," I say, and lead him forward. "Juri assigned me a driver for my stay. Seemed a waste to not use the service."

"Greetings!" Remy calls, and extends his hand to Tom. "Remy Yoshida, Mr. Quidell. It's good to meet you in person."

Tom shakes, and looks a little too pleased with himself. Remy, too, smirks.

"All right. What's going on?" They're up to something.

Remy opens the limo's rear door.

The sweet, clean scent of fresh flowers hits me before I see the blooms. I peer inside.

A huge bouquet sits in a box against the back of the front seat. A bottle of champagne and two glasses wait in another. And, hanging on the back of the seat, a nice tie and a jacket big enough for Tom.

I point. "You brought flowers? And champagne?" I look at Tom. "And a jacket?"

Remy grins. "I spoke with Mr. Quidell."

Tom laughs. "I remembered you telling me about Remy, so when he texted while you were in the shower, I answered. I wanted to make sure he knew, so he didn't come to pick you up thinking that you were going to the airport."

Remy waves us into the limo. "I hope the flowers are to your liking, Ms. Singleton."

I carefully scoot into the limo first, doing my best to mind my tight skirt, and Tom follows directly behind.

The flowers are gorgeous. Lovely blue-violet roses dot the bouquet of huge white lilies. A bright indigo ribbon bundles the stems.

The ribbon matches my skirt.

"Wow," I breathe. The softness of the petals feels as lovely on my fingertips as they look to my eyes. "How did you get this on such short notice?" Remy is a miracle worker.

Remy closes the door and climbs into the driver's seat. "It's Vegas," he says, and winks at us both.

"Thank you." I give Tom a hug. "And thank you, Remy."

He starts the limo. Tom buttons his collar and pulls the tie around his neck. By the time we reach the chapel, we have him tidy and in his new jacket. It's a bit tight across his shoulders, but most clothes are. It hangs well, though, and I thank the stars for Remy's good taste and connections.

Tom tucks a rose into the hair above my ear. "There." Gently, he strokes my cheek. "Thank you for marrying me."

I kiss his knuckles. "Thank you for being the good man you are."

A year ago, I was a lost soul treading water in waves of my own making. I hadn't realized I'd lost my footing, or more precisely, I'd never realized that I needed to find it in the first place.

Tom helped me through a flat, colorless, ugly part of my life. He's the land under my feet and I'm blessed to be marrying him.

Remy opens the door. I swing out my legs, my perfect lilies-and-roses bouquet in my hand and my wonderful soon-to-be husband at my side, and walk up the steps to a destination chapel in a city where memories are made.

Viva Las Vegas.

CHAPTER 34

Thomas

Dan sniffles on the other side of our phone connection. His fever broke yesterday, but he's still not fit to travel. The plan is for him to fly down in a few days. Sal has already promised to drive to Phoenix to fetch him.

Across the room, Sammie sits at the dining room table next to Dad. They're in an animated conversation about the national parks in the area, and the desert, and where and what she needs to research in order to "get a deep understanding of the meaning of this place."

She nods and touches his elbow, then asks about a landscape feature. It's a question that never would have crossed my mind, but now I'm thinking *How cool*. And *Wow*. And *Maybe I should take her into the mountains for our honeymoon*.

I have a feeling she'd love a camping trip in the wilds around Sedona. Sal also promised to help plan a "destination trip" once we have the new jobs—and Dad—settled.

We'll need to hold off on the planning, though. Sammie is driving back to Vegas tonight. Her flight leaves bright and early tomorrow morning. Turns out Juri Olson flies his own jet from city to city and was willing to give her a lift home.

Her environmental questions are in preparation for grilling Olson about the remote property. She wants to use the plane time to form her strategy.

My wife really is quite good at her job.

On my phone, Dan sniffles again. "You *cannot* be serious." My brother sounds more congested than incredulous. "An Elvis impersonator?"

I laugh. "Why are you surprised? It's the new family tradition." Seems Nevada has become the go-to state for Quidell weddings.

"Now what am I supposed to do? I can't afford a Tahoe wedding." He sniffles again. "And I don't think Camille has any interest in aliens."

I tip up my chin. "Hey, Dad!"

He looks over.

"Dan says he and Camille are going to get married at the Area 51 gates."

Dad rolls his eyes. "Knock it off with the dueling weddings, boys." He leans toward Sammie. "They were like this as kids, too. Always trying to one-up each other."

I lean into my phone again and address my brother. "I'm guessing you want ironic 'photography restricted in this area' and 'trespassers will be shot with extreme prejudice' wedding photos."

Dan chuckles. "Isa will charge me triple rate for that and I already told you I can't afford an expensive wedding."

Sammie throws me a big smile. "I think they should. It's not that far away. We can make it a family thing." She squeezes Dad's arm.

He visibly brightened when we pulled into the driveway. Part of me wondered if he'd thought I wasn't coming back.

It took me almost a full day, cooking a couple of family meals together, and an afternoon of him giving Sammie a tour of his studio for me to realize the truth: I don't think he expected to ever meet my new wife. I also don't think he expected her to be so much like Mom— smart, beautiful, and able to hold together his son's life.

I hadn't realized how much alike they were either, until I spent a few hours watching Sammie and Dad interact.

"Listen, Dan," I say. "Make sure you bring Camille and Bart, okay?" I think Dad needs to meet the *other* woman like Mom. Sammie and Camille are very different people with different temperaments, but their empathy and brilliance shine like the stars themselves.

"Yeah," Dan says. "Rob told me the same thing."

I'm glad my father got to meet Isa and the new proto-Quidell.

"I'll text you with flight info," Dan says. "I need to go back to bed."

"Give Bart a hug for us," I say.

Dad looks over. "A big one." The smile on his face says maybe, at least for a moment, we've gotten through the haze over his life. "Just don't spread your germs."

Dan laughs. My father smiles. Sammie looks satisfied but a little sad.

She really is empathetic and wonderful. Like Mom.

I disconnect the call and tuck my phone into my pocket. Sammie and Dad watch me walk over, and when I kiss Sammie's cheek, the same little bit of sadness I saw on her face jumps to Dad's. The same drooping around his eyes combined with the same half smile.

"You should eat before you go." Now Dad pats Sammie's elbow. "Sal made an entire vat of beef stew while you two were off making the world safe for art." He grins. "And getting Elvis-married."

Sammie smiles.

"Elvis." Dad shakes his head. "Has Tom told you how his mother and I met?"

Sammie glances at me. I've told her the story. How could I not? It's too similar to our own. I wanted her to know that I inherited more than my artistic demeanor from my dad.

She smiles at Dad. "No, he hasn't."

Dad sniffs as if he smells her little white lie. An almost-imperceptible nod follows. I think he's acknowledging this small gift she just gave him.

He leans back in his chair. "Chicago has a lot of schools and a lot of campuses," he says. "University of Chicago for her, The Art Institute for me."

Sammie also sits back in her chair.

"I was working as a bouncer at this bar downtown." He chuckles a little. "It paid well. I had my own place and I could afford tuition and supplies."

I don't know how Dad dealt with the noise and the people. Too much distraction. Too much tension. I wouldn't be able to work.

He rubs his finger along the edge of the table. "Gwen's sister, Mandy, worked at the bar. An assistant bartender, hostess, what not." He taps his finger. "She was a take-no-shit woman." He smiles and looks up. "Still is."

That's my aunt, alright.

Dad cocks his head. "One night, before it got busy, Mandy was sitting on a stool behind the bar, talking on the phone. We weren't supposed to do that, but she looked upset, so I asked."

"Mom's kitten ran away," I say.

Sammie grins.

Dad chuckles. "Gwen was quite upset."

"Mom always had a soft spot for kittens."

"She did." Dad taps the table again. "Anyway, Mandy had to take care of something—I don't remember what—so she handed me the phone."

The look on Dad's face changes. All the stress and the tension vanishes into what, to me, looks like the light cast by an angel. He's bathed in it. It's my mom's spirit.

"I had never heard a more beautiful voice in my life."

After all the years I watched my physically lovely mother harassed at soccer games, or stared at in malls, or dressing down so that she could grocery shop without some random guy hitting on her, I found it difficult to believe that my father didn't care about her looks.

But he didn't.

"We talked for two hours—until Mandy's shift was over." He chuckles again. "I was the bouncer. No one gave me shit for consoling Mandy's sister."

Dad runs his finger across the tablecloth as if sketching a picture. "I drew on a napkin the beauty I saw in her voice and I gave it to Mandy."

"Dan has the napkin, by the way," I say. I made sure it was safely protected with archival paper.

Dad nods but continues to stare at his fingers. "She came down to the bar the next night." He scoffs. "She walked in and the world moved sideways. It picked itself up, shook its worldly ass, and totally, utterly reoriented toward Gwen.

"We were married a week later." He shakes his head. "Her parents were furious. 'Too whirlwind!' her mother yelled. 'It won't last!'"

Dad looks up at the ceiling. He smiles at the memories as if they floated above his head. "Probably not the smartest thing either of us ever did, but we made it work."

Dad looks down at the tabletop in front of him. Only the ever-present hum of the AC and our breathing fills the silence.

But I think, somehow, I hear a coyote yip.

Dad takes Sammie's hand. "Don't *ever* let anyone give you crap about falling fast." He nods toward me.

He drops his hand from Sammie's and it lands on his lap. "I miss her so much."

Sammie wraps her arms around Dad's shoulders. She doesn't say anything. She offers a sincere touch.

I think that maybe the sense of art my dad has, his perception that might or might not be some type of synesthesia, takes hold. I see it in how his body relaxes—in how his face loosens and how he blinks.

He and I see the same truth in Sammie.

I think he saw the same truth in Mom, too.

He stiffens. It's pretty clear that he's had enough for one night.

Sammie lets go and leans back in her chair. "I should pack."

Dad nods and taps the table. "I'll write up that list for you." Then he turns away and buries his face in his paperwork.

Sammie takes my hand. She glances over her shoulder at Dad, her body rigid for a moment, but she shakes it off. "Help me pack, will you?"

Then she leads me away, toward the guest room. Time for my new wife to leave this realm of ghosts and return to the jungles of corporate America.

But at least I know she can handle any and all predators who might threaten her along the way.

Me, now, maybe not so much.

CHAPTER 35

Thomas

Dad sits on a tall stool in the center of his studio. It's cooler today, so I opened the doors and the transom windows. A dry breeze moves through and the sun reflects off the dirt in the yard, but he doesn't squint. He sees the truth of what's in front of him.

Seven paintings. Two completed series. One, the three "Snowbird" interpretations for the Arts Council. They're working pieces—they fall into that space between illustration and fine art. Like the strong lines and bold colors made by the artists working for the WPA during the Depression, or the posters of the Russian Revolution, Dad's three paintings have an agenda. But it's a universal human agenda, one of comfort and rest and happiness.

He painted them perfectly.

"The Council will be happy, Dad." His works will soon become part of Sedona.

He shifts his gaze to the other four pieces.

Dad discarded the black ghost painting. It now sits in the corner with his other canvases to be recycled, away from him and his finished series.

Mom's ghost moves across the four completed canvases. I think he's been painting her voice, her words, her thoughts—the dark and the light. The real and the imagined. His paintings howl with pain and sing with joy.

And they're done.

He looks up at me. "Too bad Dan and Camille couldn't stay longer."

They spent four days here. Dan and Camille took over cleaning up Dad's accounts. Bart—with his father's help—made Dad fresh snicker-doodles. Camille made the new Phoenix appointments and made Dad promise he would go, finished paintings or not. For a second, I thought she was going to make him sign a blood oath.

Everything's set. He's not to eat dinner or have anything to drink after midnight. We leave tomorrow morning and will check in around ten for his first appointment.

When he wasn't baking cookies, Bart spent all four days out in the studio with us. Dad put away Mom's ghost while the kid was here and worked on the Arts Council's commission. Bart painted his own quite literal "snow bird," featuring a snowy owl in snow against a white mountain backdrop. It's pretty damned good, for an almost six-year-old.

I told Dad I was going to pack it away with Mom's napkin.

"Yes," he'd said. "Together."

He hasn't said a lot since they left.

"Dad?"

He looks up.

"Do you want to eat?" I point at the house. "Cutoff is in two hours. No food after that, remember?" The hotel is booked. The clinic knows he's coming. I filled his car this morning and I laid out his bags for packing. "We have a long drive tomorrow."

Slowly, Dad stands. He inhales, but it looks difficult. Pain ripples across his chest and up his neck. His skin pales.

How has he been hiding the now-obvious agony? "Are you okay?" But I know—he buried it under the work. Art, the best drug.

I take his arm. His forearm feels bony. His eyes sink into his head. His skin feels as if it's going to peel off.

And I wonder if I should have thrown him into the car two weeks ago and forced him to go to the clinic. But I couldn't do that. No one can do that. It's his body and I have no say in what he does or does not do with it.

He's so fucking frail.

"Let's eat at the patio table," he says, meaning the dusty one under the overhang.

I move to help him walk over. "I'll make sandwiches."

"I can walk, son." Dad pulls himself to his full height. Slowly, he takes a cloth from his table. "I'll clean off the chairs."

I step back. The pain is still there, and now I'm wondering if it's something else. If it's more than an ache he's been hiding. "Are you okay?" I point at the house. "Dad, tell me the truth."

His eyes narrow and he sighs. "I want one of Bart's homemade snickerdoodles. I don't care if the docs say I can't have the salt and sugar. I won't be eating again for a whole day so do your father a favor and fish one out the jar."

"Dad..."

The pale leaves his skin and I swear I hear him force it away. I hear it crack and shatter under the strength of my father's will.

"We better eat the turkey before we go." He takes a slow, halting step toward the door. The table is up the walk and under the overhang, about fifteen feet from the patio door.

I move to take his arm again, but he holds up his hand.

"I can walk."

Dad takes those steps with his back straight and his shoulders square. The cloth he holds tightly in his fist. I follow close in case he needs me. In case my dad falls.

He stops next to the table and stands rigid for a moment before laying the cloth down onto the glass top. "Not too bad," he says, and makes a long, purposeful wipe. "I'll have it clean by the time you have our sandwiches ready."

The look he gives me says I'm not to argue. That I'm to go in. That I shouldn't listen to the shrill, noiseless screams erupting from my gut and into my vision. I'm to pay no heed to the oppressively hot air that's making it difficult to breathe, or to the blindingly bright glare that's making it difficult to see.

The hunting world just opened its maw.

"Dad?"

He releases the cloth but still swishes his hand, and the fabric bunches up into a little pile under his fingers. "Help me sit down."

I pull out a chair. Dad slowly descends into it.

"Thank you, son." He's staring out across the yard. His pupils are so big all I see is black. "Thank you for being here."

Dad lifts his hand as if he's reaching to touch someone's cheek. "Your mother is proud of you." He exhales sharply as if trying to breathe out all the pain. "We're proud of our sons."

"Dad?" I pull out my phone and dial 911.

He exhales one more breath and says one last word. One word full of light and wonder and, for him, life.

Right here, right in front of me, his world offers my father her hand. She'll take him away from the predators. She'll lead him out of the gullies.

"*911. What's your emergency?*"

"Gwen?" my dad mumbles. His fingers twitch. His hand falls to his lap.

"Dad?" It's the only word that forms. "Dad!" I yell.

We were going to go to the clinic tomorrow.

Everything was going to be okay.

"Dad?"

CHAPTER 36

Samantha

When I presented Jeremiah's last paintings to Juri, I swear he, like me, heard Gwen's voice. I swear he understood. "You can have what you need to get these the showings they deserve," he'd said.

I did. It's the least I could do for Jeremiah Quidell and his sons.

Now, the chill in the wind nips at my ears and I wish I'd had the foresight to put on my hat. The lake house is always cooler than home; northern Minnesota tends to be. The weather began to cool last week and we're likely to get our first hard frost tonight, but I managed to leave all my hats at home, in the loft.

Tom tells me that his father used to love the lake house. He'd bring canvases and paints and his big sketch pads when they drove up during the summer, but he never added on studio space. Never did much to the building at all.

"It's easy to breathe here," I say. It's not about working. It's about living. "It's the same reason we don't bring our computers."

Tom nods an acknowledgement. "True that." He looks over his shoulder at the house and tips his head as if he's seeing it for the first time. "I think we should start renovations in the spring." He tips his head the other way. "With a studio."

"Make sure it's big enough for you and all the little Quidells." Bart is well on his way to becoming the next great Quidell artist, and I suspect Isa's bump will one day walk a similar path.

Tom hugs me close. He doesn't say anything; we aren't going to try for a baby until next summer, after I'm established at the Olson Companies' Arts Foundation and he's made good progress on his "Desert Times" installation.

Now we lean against the rail running along the dock between the lake itself and the boathouse of his family's lake home. The evening sun shimmers over the water's surface as intense golds, oranges, and reds. Leaves in the same brilliant tones blow by. A few catch in the slats under our feet.

A turtle surfaces out in the water with a soft *plop*. The wind picks up the ring wave and pushes it toward the tall, rustling grasses next to the dock. I watch, breathing it all in, thankful to be part of the Quidell family.

Tom and Dan had their father's napkin drawing framed and they mounted it and Bart's snow bird painting over the fireplace earlier today. The napkin's lines are beginning to bleed but Jeremiah's intent is clear—he saw his future wife in the tones and modulations of her voice.

For a portrait drawn of someone he'd not yet met, it's remarkably accurate.

The scent of warmed cinnamon and sugar waft from the house. Pans and chairs rattle. Bart is helping Camille take his grandpa's favorite cookies out of the oven.

"Are you sure you want to do this?" I ask. Tom could reuse the canvases, though I understand the need for complete closure.

"Yeah," Tom says. He wraps his arm around my shoulder.

I pull my jacket tight and lean against my husband.

The wall of the boathouse jiggles and I hear muffled swearing coming from inside.

Tom chuckles. "I told him not to worry so much." He nods toward the shack.

"Dan can't help it," I say. "He's a professional." And if we're going to be playing with fire, Dan's going to make sure it's the best and safest fire around.

The house's back door opens. It groans and squeaks, and I can't help but wonder if the Quidell men will replace it when the renovations start. That door has been touched by all the Quidells—Jeremiah's parents, Tom's mom and dad, and now our generation. It would be a shame to pull it down.

Rob holds open the door as Isa walks through carrying a tripod and the camera she fitted with Jeremiah's lovely beaded strap. Tom had been adamant that she take it. He said his dad was as proud of her as he was of his sons.

"Looks like it's time," I say.

"Tom!" Dan yells. "Got the pole?"

Tom snatches the long boathook off the dock. "Right here," he answers.

The sticks at the front of the Quidell men's driftwood raft appear first, followed by the long, center support branches, and then the sticks of the back end.

Dan, Rob, and Bart—Dan and Bart, mostly, because Rob's been at school—used dry grass from the shore to tie together enough sticks and branches from the trees around the lake to make a float. Dan added a few nails here and there, and tested the wood to make sure it would burn, but not burn so well it would become a problem.

Tom hooks the float with the pole and pulls it along the shore to the open end of the dock. Quickly, he lashes it to the dock's framing.

Dan latches the door on the boathouse. He rubs his hands together and blows on his fingers as Rob and Isa navigate the walk down to the dock.

"Lake's cold," Dan says. He pulls out his phone. "Camille and Bart will be down in a second."

I pat Dan's arm and together with Rob and Isa, we walk to the open part of the dock—and the tied-down tarp behind Tom.

"Sun's setting." Rob points at the horizon. "Ready?"

The house's screen door slams. Bart, a lidded bowl in his hands and his camera around his neck, darts down the walk and jogs up the dock.

He stops next to Isa. "I have my camera set," he says as he hands his father the bowl. "See?"

It's easy to see Jeremiah in Bart. He carries the same wide Quidell shoulders, and the same bright light.

Isa bends over and checks Bart's camera. "Looks good, but I want you to take a few test shots to make sure you're happy with this setting, okay? If you don't like it, change it."

"Okay, Auntie Isa." Bart scurries between the adults so that he has a clear shot of the lake.

Isa watches him go. "I'm surprised he hasn't lost interest in that camera yet."

"I'm not," Tom says. "He gravitates toward form and structure."

Dan scoffs and throws his arm around Camille as she walks up. "What are we going to do with that kid?"

Exactly what you are doing now, I think. Bart's a lucky boy.

We're all lucky, and me maybe the most of all. I have Tom.

"Help me with the tarp," he says.

Rob undoes the corner closest to him, and Dan the corner by his foot. The wind catches the tarp, and blue flashes. The plastic snaps, but Tom pulls it in.

Underneath, sitting on the dock, is his massive dream painting with the primordial plants, the concourses, and the wolf-like figures.

He never did go back to it. When we returned from taking care of his father's estate, he stared at it for almost an hour. Just sat in front of it until he didn't anymore. It's been in the corner facing the wall ever since.

Centered on top of Tom's dream painting sits one his father started. Tom called it his dad's black ghost painting. Said his dad moved on from it. That it, like Tom's huge dream painting, was a stepping stone.

They're not misfires, or mis-starts, he said. They're a veil that needed to be passed through.

Even now with it sitting on top of Tom's, Jeremiah's ghost painting gives me chills. Dan and Rob refuse to look at it. Camille refuses to allow Bart to get a good look.

And I think Tom is correct. That it's time to send both these works home. Let the world take them.

Tom, Rob, and Dan carefully set both paintings on the raft. Isa and Bart snap pictures.

Tom steps back. "I've been thinking about what to say." He looks around at his family. "About what Dad might want me to say."

He rubs his face. It's still raw for him. Even now, after all the legal work and me starting at the Olson Companies and him officially becoming a professional artist, after me setting up the deal with Juri to get Jeremiah's final paintings into the Vegas galleries, after the memorial in Sedona and the one in Minneapolis, Tom's breathing still hitches. His eyes still mist.

I tell him it will take time. He knows. Dan and Rob know. We all understand.

"Dad taught me what it means to feel the art." He points at the paintings. "Instead of letting the art feel you." His eyebrows bunch up. "It's not easy."

Next to me, Isa nods her agreement. Dan squeezes Bart's shoulder.

"This is for Dad," Tom says. He nods toward Bart first, then toward Isa. Then, with a smile, he nods toward me. "But it's also for the family."

Rob and Dan each offer Tom a hug. They squeeze each other's shoulders, and when they step back, I think all three stand taller.

"Okay, little man," Dan says. "Got your cookies?"

Bart takes the bowl from Camille. "Grampa liked snickerdoodles." He dutifully walks between the adults, offering each a cookie. He stays away from the paintings, more, I think, because Camille told him to than for any other reason. The emotions infecting the art aren't part of his young life. The haunting, the fear. To him, they're just scary pictures.

When he stops in front of me, I lift one of the warm, sugary cookies from his bowl. "Thank you," I say. "These smell wonderful, Bart. You did a good job."

He beams at me, then I think he realizes he's supposed to be solemn. "Thank you, Auntie Sammie." He gives me a quick hug.

Dan tosses a piece of cookie onto the paintings. Camille follows, then Bart, Rob, and Isa.

"Thank you, Jeremiah," I whisper, and toss my bit of love and warmth onto the two abandoned paintings.

Next to me, Tom tosses his crumb. It bounces a little, and lands on top of his mother's ghost.

A low, pained chuckle rises from his chest. Then he turns away.

Dan strikes a match. The flame flares up, a spiral of brightness in the dimming evening light. A spark wisps out into the air, and the strong scent of ash follows.

The match lands in the center of the ghost painting. Rob strikes his own, and it too lands on his father's piece. Tom's lands on the wolf-like figure.

Rob unlashes the raft as the paintings begin to snap. Sparks flick out as the flames catch. The dock begins to glow, and warmth rolls through the chill in the air.

Tom uses the boat hook to push the raft away from the dock and out toward the center of the lake.

Bart snaps a few more photos. Isa, with Rob's help, makes sure her shots are what she wants. Dan takes Camille's hand.

I lean against Tom's shoulder again. "I think Jeremiah would have liked this."

Tom inhales and exhales hard, the way someone trying to cover a thumping heart or a clenching stomach breathes. "Yeah, I think they both would."

Bart appears, his bowl of cookies in hand. "Have another cookie, Uncle Tommy."

"Thanks, Bart," he says, and weaves his fingers through mine before taking another bite.

Watch for the future **Quidell Brothers** titles

Andrew's Kiss
and
Daniel's Vows

Coming soon

THE WORLDS OF
KRIS AUSTEN RADCLIFFE

Hot Contemporary Romance:

The Quidell Brothers
Thomas's Muse
Daniel's Fire
Robert's Soul
Thomas's Need
Andrew's Kiss *(coming soon)*

Genre-bending Science Fiction about
love, family, and dragons:

WORLD ON FIRE
Series one
Fate Fire Shifter Dragon
Games of Fate
Flux of Skin
Fifth of Blood

Bonds Broken & Silent
All But Human
Men and Beasts
The Burning World

Series Two
Witch of the Midnight Blade
Call of the Dragonslayer (*coming soon*)

Smart Urban Fantasy:

<u>Northern Creatures</u>
Monster Born
Vampire Cursed
Elf Raised
Wolf Hunted (*coming soon*)

ABOUT THE AUTHOR

As a child, Kris took down a pack of hungry wolves with only a hard-cover copy of *The Dragonriders of Pern* and a sharpened toothbrush. That fateful day set her on a path traversing many storytelling worlds —dabbles in film and comic books, time as a talent agent and a textbook photo coordinator, and a foray into nonfiction. After co-authoring *Mind Shapes: Understanding the Differences in Thinking and Communication*, Kris returned to academia. But she craved narrative and a richly-textured world of Fates, Shifters, and Dragons—and unexpected, true love.

Kris lives in Minnesota with her husband, two daughters, Handsome Cat, and an entire menagerie of suburban wildlife bent on destroying her house. That battered-but-true copy of *Dragonriders*? She found it yesterday. It's time to pay a visit to the woodpeckers.

Fore more information
www.krisaustenradcliffe.com
krisradcliffe@sixtalonsign.com

www.ingramcontent.com/pod-product-compliance
Lightning Source LLC
Chambersburg PA
CBHW07045726062
47161CB00004B/1343